ZOMBIE DAWN
EXODUS

MICHAEL G. THOMAS
& NICK S. THOMAS

ISBN 978-1906512590

Typeset by Swordworks Books
Printed and bound in the UK & US
A catalogue record of this book is available from the British Library

Cover design by Swordworks Books
www.swordworks.co.uk

ZOMBIE DAWN
EXODUS

CHAPTER ONE

RV MOREAU, NORTHERN PACIFIC OCEAN

The Research Vessel Moreau was a Thomas G. Thompson-class research vessel that had originally been built for use by the US Navy. In the last six years she had been bought by the company for use as an off-shore research vessel as part of its wider activities. At nearly a hundred metres she was a substantial vessel and currently carried a crew, research staff and security detachment of sixty four people. She was equipped with two rigid-hull inflatable rescue/work boats onboard, as well as a single submersible and a retrofitted helipad. Built into the hull were ROV and submersible hangars, a fully equipped machine shop and a custom built medical lab and clinic.

Deep inside the vessel a team of scientists were busy studying the details of a new subject on their computer terminals. The computer monitors showed a detailed schematic of an ocean liner. The first screen showed a side on view that displayed the ship's profile, whilst the screens either side showed figures on estimated size, displacement and course information. Another monitor gave a heavily magnified live feed of the vessel in the currently calm waters of the North Pacific Ocean.

Daniels, one of the technicians, ran through various databases to check the configuration against all known vessels.

"Yeah, here she is," he said as he popped up the ship's details on another screen.

Clarkson, another technician sat in his rotating chair as he read the specification out to the annoyance of some of the other staff in the room.

"She's a Cunard Line ocean liner, the RMS Mauretania 2. She's nearly four hundred metres long and has a combined crew and passenger capacity of just under five thousand people. According to the last information available she was on a world cruise thirteen months ago. Two months after Z-Day there is information from the coast guard that she was spotted off Hawaii, nothing since," said Clarkson.

Dr Garcia entered the room and moved straight up to the main screen.

"The Mauretania? Interesting," she said quietly to herself.

She hit a few keys, bringing up detailed schematics of

parts of the ship before turning to the two technicians.

"I wonder what's she doing out here. Is there any information on her from the rest of the flotilla?" she asked.

Clarkson shrugged and then turned back to his display. Daniels however had already connected to the flotilla.

"Nothing from them either. I have them checking the satellite data they downloaded last week. Maybe they'll find something there," he answered.

"Have you picked up any communication or signal from her yet?" she continued, speaking directly to Daniels who seemed the more competent of the two.

Daniels double checked his system before turning round, "No, nothing. No sign of communication, power or movement. She's dead in the water."

"Hold on, look at this!" said Clarkson.

"What do you have?" replied an intrigued Dr Garcia.

"Well, if we zoom in here it looks like there are burn marks and damage in these places. They look like the observation decks near the dining areas."

On the screen to his right the schematics popped up showing the crew and passenger areas of the massive liner. Clarkson certainly seemed to be correct as the external damage appeared to be related to the most used and populated parts of the ship.

"Also, look here," he said as he pressed the mouse button.

The three dimensional model rotated around to show the upper decks of the ship. There should have been banks of boats lined up but instead at least half of the boats were missing. Of the boats that remained some of them were hanging at odd angles, as though people were halfway through using them when they were stopped. There were also at least three boats hanging from the cranes that would have lowered them into the water in an emergency.

Dr Garcia examined the screens in details, concentrating on the boats in particular.

"So, something made them abandon ship. I think we can all guess what that might have been," she said in a humourless tone.

"The next questions are when did this happen and where are the people that escaped?" she asked rhetorically.

A low buzz echoed across the room as the ship's public address system activated.

"Dr Garcia, please report to the briefing room," came the message.

With a shake of her head the doctor hit a few keys, sending a job to the printers nearby. She stood up and collected the paperwork as she headed for the door. Just a few feet before leaving the room she turned back and called over to the technicians.

"We need more information on her. Send me a message when the drone is over the ship. I need data and the direct video feed for the meeting ASAP. Got it?" she asked in a firm tone.

"Yes, Ma'am," came the reply.

Dr Garcia left the room and headed along the short corridor that led to the command part of the ship. Since being taken on by the company it had been expanded and improved to offer greater space for personnel and computer equipment at the expense of the cranes and normal heavy equipment. A man in combat fatigues and carrying an automatic carbine followed her at a short distance.

Dr Garcia approached the door to the briefing room, the heavy metal door was flanked by two men in suits, each was visibly armed with Heckler & Koch MP7 submachine guns. As she reached the men the one to the right whispered into his intercom and then pushed the door open. He nodded at her as she entered the room and shut it behind her with an audible clunk. In front of her was a large oval table that seated a dozen people from a variety of backgrounds. At the head of the table was the director and now leader of what was left of the research company, Mr Morton. He smiled as he watched her entrance.

"Ah, welcome, Dr Garcia," he turned to the rest of the room, "as you know, Dr Garcia is head of our research and development operations within the flotilla and one of the founding members of the Hawaii Sanctuary due to her..."

Dr Garcia gave him an odd look as he continued.

"...rather specialist knowledge," he added in a cautious tone.

She took her place at the table and glanced around at the others who were there. Of the dozen people she noted they were the usual heads of departments, but there were a few new faces. Opposite her was Captain Mathius, the vessel's chief of security. He always wore combat fatigues and was never seen without at least a pistol on his side. Sitting next to him were two people she didn't recognise.

"I have important information on the new vessel we've been tracking," she started but was immediately interrupted by Mr Morton.

"Please, we'll get on to that important concern shortly. First of all I have a few company announcements to make."

Mr Morton stood up and walked to the banks of displays at the end of the room.

"As most of you know, we have been tracking several vessels over the last few weeks. Dr Garcia has some important news on our latest find. We'll get to that in just a moment. Before I start I would like to welcome our two newest members, Dr Willis and Ms Price, both experts in genetics, who arrived yesterday," he said.

The two stood up, looking to the group and then to Mr Morton.

"Thank you, Mr Morton. On behalf of the Biotech ST

Corporation, we appreciate your swift actions in the last week to extract our personnel from our laboratory," spoke Dr Willis.

They sat down, with Ms Price being surprisingly silent, Mr Morton continued.

"As you know, since the outbreak we have travelled along the Canadian and US coasts picking up specialists and experts wherever we can to add to the growing flotilla. Last week Captain Mathius led a unit to the BSTC research station off the coast of Northern California," he said as he pressed a number of buttons on a remote control.

A map of North America popped up showing the landmass details in a series of colours from white to purple. Mr Morton moved closer to the screen, pointing at the coast.

"Most of you are aware of our current status in this disaster. For those of you that have only recently joined us this briefing will update you on what we know so far, and also on our strategy for the future."

The screen at the end of the room filled with a set of charts showing populations, casualty and infection figures. Mr Morton continued.

"We now have enough information to start forming a realistic picture of what happened and what is happening in this pandemic. Casualty reports show that in the first six weeks the outbreak took all the inhabited areas of the West Coast," he pointed at a band of purple, "only small groups survived in the more rural areas or held out in isolated areas."

The display zoomed in to the coastal region where most of the area showed in purple with a few red and lighter colours sprinkled about.

"With the collapse of the national infrastructure, and the overrunning of all urban centres, we have been assessing data from those countries still able to communicate with us. The current estimate for this region is that there are about fifty thousand survivors left on the entire Western seaboard," he said sternly.

There was an audible gasp in the room. Mr Morton paused for a moment whilst the news sank in.

"It gets worse though. Data from the rest of North America and throughout Europe and Asia shows us that the spread of the infection has been exponential. There are no known cities left inhabited on the planet and the average survival rate is roughly a tenth of one percent."

"So only one in a thousand has survived after just a year?" asked one of the men in a dark suit.

"Correct," answered Mr Morton.

He pressed a few more buttons and the display zoomed in to the United Kingdom.

"Of our three facilities in the UK, only one remains and that is based in the North Sea on Alpha Twelve platform. The first two were overrun in the first week with no survivors."

The map zoomed out to show the whole of the country.

"From the last known satellite passes, and the contact that remains with parts of the country, we can ascertain that the survival rate is roughly half of that of the United States. We are putting this down to the reduced access to firearms and the high population density of the country. We are in contact with a small number of communities in these regions along the Welsh and Scottish borders."

Mr Morton zoomed the map out further to show a view of the entire globe. Most of it was marked in the purple colour that indicated maximum infection and minimal survival chances.

"As you can see, the entire world is affected. Japan has suffered terrible losses, with most survivors taking refuge on the smaller islands or escaping in ships. Many of these are looking to join the Southern Pacific Flotilla that is assembling. The rest of Europe and Asia is in a similar situation. More importantly, things are not getting better."

There was almost complete silence in the room as the group digested what had been said.

Captain Mathius signalled to Mr Morton before standing up.

"The security situation has stabilised for us now that we have the resources of the Sanctuary. The flotilla currently includes over twenty vessels at any one time, with many more being escorted to Hawaii when time and resources allow it. As well as our current complement of research vessels and transports we have also been joined by the USS Harpers Ferry, an amphibious transport vessel that is equipped with a small complement of Marines on board, as well as helicopters and hovercraft. This vessel can provide critical aerial coverage as well as a significant amphibious landing capability. Captain Black is in charge of the Marine Unit."

Captain Mathius signalled to the young man who stood up quickly.

"If you could explain the position of the military right now?" he asked.

The young officer nodded in acknowledgment.

"As you may be aware, most combat units were heavily engaged in operations in the first few weeks of the outbreak. With just a few exceptions these resulted in heavy casualties and the abandonment of most facilities. Warships lack either the personnel or supplies to stay operational and have been abandoned in port, apart from small numbers that are operating independently. We estimate that of the approximately two hundred and fifty ships, less than ten are active and each with reduced crews and capabilities. Food, fuel, people and ammunition are scarce and needed to keep communities alive," he explained.

"My unit was almost completely wiped out in Afghanistan at the start of this. Since then I have moved through four different combat zones and seen most of my men killed. The troops on board our ship are all that is left of these units. Twelve months ago I was a Sergeant, now I am a Captain. Our last orders were to provide assistance where we can and to help US citizens re-establish themselves as quickly as possible."

Dr Garcia spoke before anybody else could join in.

"Captain Black, what is your ship's status? Are you able to conduct operations?" she asked.

Captain Black looked at her carefully, curious as to the question.

"Our ship is in good condition and well run by the crew. We have a reduced Marine detachment of nearly one hundred men, all experienced, well equipped and armed. Ammunition supplies are good for now, though we always need to secure new sources of ammunition. We have two hovercraft and two helicopters onboard, though we use those sparingly as parts are a problem. We are able to conduct operations. Why? Did you have something in mind?" he asked.

Dr Garcia smiled at the Marine before turning back to Mr Morton.

"May I?" she asked.

Mr Morton nodded and returned to his seat.

"There are two pieces of urgent news to deal with. The first is that we have some results on the development of the antidote drugs. No, we don't have a cure but we can hold off the effects for almost a week, providing the drug is taken daily," she explained.

"What is the other piece of news?" asked one of the scientists.

"We have found a substantial vessel approximately an hour away from our current position," she said.

There was a sense of excitement in the room as each person looked around. Dr Garcia continued.

She's the Cunard Cruise Liner Mauretania 2. This ship has been out of contact for some time and finding her was quite a surprise. She's dead in the water and it looks like she's been abandoned, though that is unconfirmed. We have a UAV on its way and it should be providing data shortly. There's a chance we might find survivors but an even greater chance that we can find fuel, supplies and possibly intelligence from her.

"Ah, I see," said Captain Black, finally understanding the reasoning behind her question.

Mr Morton took his place at the head of the table as the rest turned their attention back to him.

"So as you can see, the general situation is not good but we are making cautious strides in turning things around for those that are left. The Sanctuary is secure and the flotilla is making slow gains in people and supplies. After speaking with the newly formed council we are confident of a return to some form of normality in the next few years," he said.

"Normality? What do you mean?" asked Dr Willis.

Well, it is our intention to continue looking for survivors

and to start work on re-establishing compounds in secure areas over a period of time. The Sanctuary proved it can be done and we intend on recreating this success elsewhere.

"How soon?" asked a sceptical Dr Willis.

"Well, that depends on several key things. The first of these is how many people we can actually find and save. The more we find the quicker we can start. The second is how successful we are on setting up regions that are safe and secure."

"Aren't we forgetting about the elephant in the room?" asked Captain Black.

"The zombies?" asked Dr Garcia.

Captain Black nodded before continuing. "I've fought against these things in the open, at night, in the day, in cities and even on board ships. They do not tire, do not seem to actually need to eat and will not stop. The last town I saw put up one hell of a fight, but in the end each casualty they took simply increased the enemy's numbers. What started as a few thousand people against a few hundred zombies turned into seven people trying to escape from a town overrun by thousands of zombies. We have tracked them moving hundreds of miles to find the living, even crossing rivers and deep lakes."

Mr Morton raised his hands, looking for silence.

"I understand your concerns and you are of course correct. Make no mistake, these creatures have brought us to the edge, and I mean the edge, of disaster. We cannot however let this hold us back from our greater purpose of re-establishing our authority over this planet. We will of course start off small, just as many small groups are trying throughout the world. Already we know of at least seven groups in Europe, all working to rebuild small communities. In Australia we've heard rumours of nomadic convoys travelling the deserts and this has been repeated in the wilderness of Northern Asia. We will be careful and build in as many safeguards as we can."

He turned to Captain Black whilst hitting a series of keys.

"You are right about the undead. The battle for New York lasted three weeks, and even with the intervention of over twenty thousand soldiers, airmen and marines the city fell with a loss of millions. This was repeated in most of the major cities across the country and the failed confrontations simply drained our resources away from evacuation."

Mr Morton brought up the screen that showed Hawaii.

"The Sanctuary is an archipelago of eight major islands, several atolls and numerous smaller islets. In the first weeks of the outbreak the undead broke into the general population on the five largest islands. The casualties were severe but due to the substantial military presence there, all but Oahu were retaken. The population of the islands was quickly knocked down from over a million to just under two thousand, but this has stabilised. We have established new research facilities on the islands and are working on functional housing, farms and factories to eventually provide the things we need to get back on our feet. After the undead outbreak through the United States most of the combat units and ships redeployed to help where they could, and this has resulted in only a small military presence being retained on the islands."

Dr Garcia looked agitated as she received a message to her PDA device. She read the details carefully whilst Mr Morton continued describing the status of the Sanctuary. The PDA message was an update about the Cunard liner and that the UAV was about to reach the vessel. Hitting a button she stood up, interrupting Mr Morton.

"Mr Morton, the UAV is in range and we have a live feed of the ship," she said.

"Put it through," said Mr Morton as he sat down.

Dr Garcia stepped forward, pressing a few buttons to transfer the video feed to the main screen. With several flashes the feed appeared, showing three different views from the autonomous vehicle. One image was a thermal display, whilst the other two were short and long range cameras. On the long range displays the ship could be seen in all her glory.

"Any damage, it doesn't look bad from here?" asked Captain Black.

With a flicker the second display zoomed in closely to the ship, the detail was very fine and picked out the doors and windows on the upper hull, as well as the damage to boats and life rafts that were only half lowered. Dr Garcia tapped on her PDA and moved the camera down onto several key parts of the ship. The first was the deck near the bow where what looked like scores of boxes and cases were scattered. Nearby were barrels and liquid containers, some were still tied down with cables to pallets.

"Looks like somebody was trying to unload her, possibly some of the fuel," said Dr Willis.

The thermal camera showed heat activity at several key points on the ship. One was near the stern whilst the rest were close to one of the large function rooms.

"Interesting," said Captain Black. "The heat could be from fires or potentially from areas that are still occupied."

"What is her complement?" asked Mr Morton.

"Approximately five thousand, but we don't have the figures for her last voyage," answered Dr Garcia.

"I've seen enough. We'll continue this meeting tomorrow morning. Captain Mathius, Captain Black, Dr Garcia, if you could wait behind."

The rest of the people stood up and after packing away their papers made their way to the guarded door. Once alone, Mr Morton continued.

"We need firm intelligence on that vessel. I need the three of you to organise a reconnaissance operation to the Mauretania 2. For now I just need information, but be prepared for survivors. If you find anybody you will of course observe standard quarantine procedures. Captain Mathius, I'm putting you in charge of this operation, you will handle things from here. I want Captain Black and Dr Garcia on the operation."

"I'm sorry, I don't need a civilian on this operation," objected Captain Black.

"Captain Black, perhaps you could be a little more condescending? I have been on scores of operations and have faced these creatures on multiple occasions. My technical and biological research expertise is unparalleled. You aren't going without me!"

Mr Morton raised an eyebrow in amusement at the verbal exchange.

"As Dr Garcia has explained, she is our most experienced and knowledgeable person. She will assist in an advisory capacity. Understood?" he asked.

Captain Black raised his hands in defeat.

"It's your operation, and we'll play it your way, for now."

"Very good. I will leave you to your planning, report back to me when you have news," said Mr Morton, as he moved to the door. He turned to them just before he left.

"Just be careful out there, those things bite!" he said with a mischievous look.

CHAPTER TWO

NEW SOUTH WALES, AUSTRALIA
8.15AM

The heat beating down on the RV brought Bruce to a clammy and unwanted awakening. He'd become accustomed to sleeping in thick canvas tenting, a far more comfortable experience than the modern enclosed ways of sleeping outdoors these days. The thick canvas stopped the sun super heating the tent, and the air flow kept it fresh and comfortable. Bruce groaned as he sat up on the bed. He was in a thirty seven foot RV, a motor home, shared with four other survivors.

Bruce wiped his brow, sweat had already begun dripping down his face. He was dehydrated from the many beers the night before. Opening the curtains nearest him, Bruce peered out across the open plain, along the line of vehicles.

This was their regular routine for nights now, simply park up in a line on whichever road they were driving, in as open an area as possible. The beers the night before were considered by most of the group to be vital to the morale of the survivors. Bruce, who had fallen into the role of leader, told everyone to treat each day like a road trip.

He peered through the window then shuffled around, peering out of the other windows. All he could see was a line of vehicles behind him, and sand and asphalt to the side and front. Bruce got to the main door of the vehicle and slid across the three bolts that were spaced evenly top to bottom. The security of an RV may have been good enough to keep out the odd thief, but that was then and this was now. All of their vehicles had received substantial armour and safeguards.

The door of the lead vehicle swung open and Bruce stumbled out, he was wearing torn jeans, a faded Motorhead t-shirt and flip flops. Bruce liked to think of himself as a rock star on tour whenever he could, it kept him from depression. He unzipped his trousers and sighed as he finally began to water the sand. Looking down the line of vehicles, he could already see several people following his example.

"Morning, boss!" shouted Dylan.

Bruce looked back to his friend who was sitting in a camping chair on the roof of their RV. All of the larger vehicles in the convoy now had roof hatches and ladders to them. Each night every other vehicle would post a watch on the roof. In total, the convoy consisted of six RVs, four 4x4s that were all Land Cruisers, and a Road Train. The Road Train truck had been converted to an RV by having a caravan body fitted onto the back, but it still towed fuel containers. Fuel was highly important to their way of life, but fortunately it was still available in large quantities. The survivors took any fuel they could at every opportunity.

"Gooday, fool!" shouted Bruce.

"Hey, Bruce, want some breakfast?" called Brooke from their vehicle.

"Yeah, bacon and eggs!" shouted Bruce.

She laughed, but it was far from a new joke by the fatigued leader. They tried to continue a life of fun and camaraderie, but it was many of the little things in life they now missed, largely many of the perishable goods.

"How's some beef jerky and a coffee suit you?" asked Brooke.

"Have to do, won't it!" said Bruce.

"Yep!" said Brooke.

"Hey, Connor, get on the radio, tell the chiefs to meet here in ten minutes!" shouted Bruce.

"Okidoki!" Connor replied.

Connor was still lying in bed. He'd only woken up just seconds before at the sound of the shouting, but hadn't had any motivation to get up. He went over to the radio and called in Bruce's message to the chiefs. The term 'chief' was one that Bruce had coined for the person in charge of each vehicle. He'd always considered it important that each unit within a larger group have their sub-commanders, no different to an office or an army.

Bruce climbed back aboard his vehicle and sat down at the dining table. He ripped open the bag of beef jerky and began to chew away on the tough meat. He could only dream of fresh bacon and eggs, the luxuries that were long gone, but not forgotten. He'd always preferred tea to coffee, but powdered milk was disgusting, he'd rather drink coffee than stoop that low.

Ten minutes later the chiefs climbed aboard and sat down with Bruce. The navigators of the trucks stood beside them. They had this meeting each morning to assess their location, supplies and intentions for the day. A lot can change in a day, and therefore they always kept up this routine. The supplies, in terms of people, equipment, food and water were equally spread between the larger vehicles to ensure that a loss of a vehicle did not significantly affect their resources. The Land Train towed by far the largest amount of fuel, but all of the vehicles in the convoy carried a sizeable number of fuel cans.

"Morning to you all, Brooke, more coffee for everyone please!" said Bruce.

"What's the plan, boss?" asked Damian.

"Honestly, I'm a little bored of driving, we have a

reasonable amount of supplies, let's take a day off, we haven't done it in weeks," said Bruce.

"You sure?" asked Keith.

"Yeah fuck it, the supplies aren't going anywhere, certainly not in a day, we've got a nice open plain here, let's get a game going, relax and enjoy ourselves," said Bruce.

Connor and Dylan were listening intently from the roof, pretending to be keeping watch but focusing all their attention on eavesdropping.

"Alright, but tomorrow we need to be on the move," said Keith.

"What did I just say? I said take a day off, not pitch up for the week," said Bruce.

"Fair enough," said Keith.

"Okay, all agreed?" asked Bruce.

The group smiling and nodding all agreed.

"Connor! Lay out a pitch and find the ball!" shouted Bruce.

"Fucking ey!" shouted Connor.

"Right gents, four guards at any one time, cycle your people, meeting adjourned. Let's enjoy ourselves a little," said Bruce.

Half an hour later a rough football pitch had been fashioned on the sandy dirt beside the road and seven men aside were about to begin playing. The rest of the convoy's people were either on guard on the roofs of the RVs or sitting in the shade beside them.

The goals were jackets spaced roughly the right distance apart, it was a shirts and skins game. Bruce had joined in, he never really was much into football, but the opportunity to just forget all their woes and enjoy himself was something he could not resist, even if he would look like a muppet.

The lazy crowd cheered on from the sidelines, not ever getting up from their camp chairs and stools, except for food and water. The game played on, players cycling in and out from the side until after three hours, there was nobody left with the will to play. Most of the group slept through the afternoon after exerting themselves in the heat, it was dark when Bruce woke up.

Yet again, he stumbled to his feet and looked over to the table in his RV. Brooke, Connor and Dylan were watching a movie, he got up and walked over to them.

"What the fuck are you watching?" asked Bruce.

"Love Actually," said Brooke.

"You bunch of nancies," said Bruce.

"Fuck you!" said Brooke.

"Not you, them! You're supposed to be zombie slaying action stars, not gay fuck muppets!" said Bruce.

"Haven't you ever considered the fact that all the action and violence we've seen over the last year is enough, that perhaps when we don't have to be fighting we don't want to watch more?" asked Brooke.

Bruce was taken aback by the comment, and he actually

thought about it for a minute. It was indeed true, he played football for the very same reason, and that was a gay game, so why not watch a chick's movie and enjoy it for what it was, peaceful. He may have thought it, but he'd never admit it.

"You bunch of poofters!" said Bruce.

He walked out of the RV to the delightful sight of a roaring fire. It wasn't needed for heat, but the light was soothing, and he knew full well the naturally relaxing nature that fire had on human beings. Bruce had spent many weekends before the Zompoc sat around a campfire, an experience he'd always enjoyed.

"Right, get the grog out!" shouted Bruce.

Ten people were gathered around the fire, out of a total of forty six. It always felt like a good size group to be part of, but when Bruce stopped to consider the fact that they were some of the very lucky and capable few who were still human, it was depressing. They carried on drinking throughout the night without incident. The group called themselves The Wanderers, after one of Jake's favourite songs. He'd been a steady character throughout their first year of survival, still driving his battered old Ford F150.

All of the group's vehicles were heavily outfitted with armour and protection, with thick roo bars or improvised rams on the fronts and mesh grills over all windows. They rarely saw a zombie during their camping, because they always made camp in isolated and desolate lands.

However, they knew for a fact that if they stayed long enough in any one place that some number of creatures would always find them.

Since the first few days of the Zompoc beginning Bruce had always made it his mission in life to face the zombies on his terms, at a time and location of his choice, because too often they had been forced into deadly situations.

The following day the group once again set out in their convoy, heading for the outskirts of a nearby city, looking to forage anything useful that they could find, as they had become so accustomed to doing. Twenty five miles down the road, Connor called Bruce to the front of the vehicle where he was at the wheel.

"Bruce, one of the RVs behind us is all over the road," he said.

Bruce looked in the driver's side mirror. He could see the wagon veering across the road. This was not at all in keeping with their strict manner of working.

"Dylan, get on the radio and find out what the fuck is happening with that RV, it looks like Rattlesnake," said Bruce.

Each of the vehicles had a name, not just to create a bond and attachment for its crew, but also a designation to keep things simple and clear when discussing convoy formations and tactics and logistics.

"Rattlesnake, this is Road Hog, come in," said Dylan.

"This is Rattlesnake, Jackson is at the wheel and he's

been drinking, he's pretty off it, over," said Christian.

"Give me the handset!" said Bruce.

"Tell him to put the fucking bottle down and let someone else take over, over!" shouted Bruce.

"I already told him that boss, he's wild," said Christian.

"I'm bringing the convoy to a stop, over," said Bruce.

"Connor, bring us to a halt, slowly," he ordered.

Connor slowed the group down to a stop and Bruce was immediately out the door and onto the hot asphalt. Before he could step any further down the convoy to sort the mess out, Rattlesnake pulled out of the convoy and accelerated down the line. Bruce flailed his arms about, furious.

"Jackson! Stop the fucking vehicle!" shouted Bruce.

It had no effect, the big RV stormed past him. Jake pulled up with his battered old truck beside Bruce.

"Bruce, what's going on?" asked Jake.

"That idiot is off his face!" Bruce replied.

"Jump in!" shouted Jake.

Bruce jumped into the truck bed, thankful of the old man's help just as he had been a year before. The v8 rumbled as Jake followed on after the RV. Bruce stood up in the back of the truck, holding onto the roll bar running over the cab.

"Pull up alongside the driver's side!" shouted Bruce.

They were nearing Rattlesnake when it swerved off to the side the road, a wheel clipping a rock and sending it onto two wheels before slamming to the dirt on its side and sliding for thirty feet. Jake slammed the brakes and slid to a halt not far behind it.

"Fuck me!" shouted Bruce.

"What do you want me to do?" asked Jake,

"Radio Road Hog, tell them to bring the convoy up, we've got some mess to sort out! And tell them we may need some medical attention," said Bruce.

He jumped off the back of the truck and ran over to the crashed RV. Bruce could already hear the groans of agony from inside, at least that meant they were alive. These vehicles were built to be completely sealed from zombies, and therefore were not at all easy to get into. He got up alongside the roof, the hatch on top being the easiest thing for him to reach.

"Christian, Christian! Open the roof hatch!" screamed Bruce.

There was no reply, all Bruce could hear was the sound of Jake talking to the convoy on his radio. Finally Bruce could hear the sound of someone stumbling around inside the RV.

"Christian, open the hatch!" shouted Bruce.

The bolt slid across and the roof hatch swung open. Christian had blood dripping down his face and was cradling his left arm, he was battered and bloody.

"How is everyone else?" asked Bruce.

"Jackson is unconscious up front, Carly and Jack are

down on the floor, I think Carly's leg is broken, Jack is just bashed about," said Christian.

"What a fucking idiot!" shouted Bruce.

The first vehicles of the convoy pulled up alongside them on the road by Jake's truck. Five people ran to the aid of the stricken vehicle, those with first aid or medical experience.

"Jake, you and Dylan organise security, I don't want any more surprises!" said Bruce.

"No problem!" shouted Jake.

Jake looked at the people who had gathered before him, doing their jobs correctly and in good order. He was pleased that after such a display of stupidity and poor discipline the majority were carrying on as they should in these circumstances.

"Right, you're going to have to get inside and take care of them there, I'll start arranging recovery of the vehicle," said Bruce.

The five helpers nodded in response and began climbing in through the roof hatch. Bruce made his way back up to the road to where Jake stood.

"Sentries are out, we're all sorted," said Jake.

"Good job. Now, let's talk about getting this vehicle back on its feet," said Bruce.

"You want to recover it?" asked Jake.

"Yeah, it's a good vehicle and it's had quite a bit of time put into setting it up right. I don't see any reason why we can't get it back on the road in no time. Will the trucks be able to pull it over or will you need something heavier?" said Bruce.

"I guess if we get three of the trucks up here we'll manage it," said Jake.

"Alright, get on it," said Bruce.

He looked back at the vehicle resting on its side, people clambering through the roof hatch.

"What a complete fuck up," said Bruce.

He stumbled back towards his vehicle, now parked fifty feet from the crash site. Bruce stepped up into the vehicle and opened the onboard fridge. A beer was what he needed right now, the heat and stress of the crappy morning being too much. Any sensible leader would have kept strict rules on alcohol in the Zombie Apocalypse, but not Bruce. He climbed up the ladder to the roof where Dylan was sitting.

"How's it going, mate?" asked Dylan.

Bruce sat down near Dylan, his feet hanging over the edge of the vehicle.

"Not too great," said Bruce.

"What's up?" asked Dylan.

"Look at this mess. We were lucky this time that such stupidity happened in a safe area. Next time it could be the end of all of us," said Bruce.

"But this was an accident, right?" asked Dylan.

"Not really, we treat life like a party, it's hardly surprising that we should then suffer the same crap that party nuts always do," said Bruce.

Bruce knocked back his cool beer, fully aware of the contradictory nature of his words and actions. He thought about the dangerous line they walked and the risks they took. Apart from the careful and well planned image that they generally presented, the group was gun hoe and took too many risks. Despite this, he wondered if there was any other way. Humanity had never managed to rid itself of vices such as alcohol, tobacco and gambling when it was at its peak, how then could they be expected to be any better?

The more Bruce thought about it, the more his head hurt. Perhaps he didn't do things the best way possible, but they were at least still alive, and perhaps actually getting some enjoyment out of life was more important than doing everything perfectly and safely.

Twenty minutes later the three trucks were hitched up to the crashed vehicle. They had decided to leave the survivors and first aiders inside, have them hold on rather than escape through the roof hatch, which was not easily accessible the way vehicle lay on its side.

"Ready?" shouted Jake.

"Yeah, put some power down, but take it easy!" shouted Bruce.

The dirty and battered trucks slowly edged forward, taking up the slack on the ropes until they finally pulled taut. Eventually the stricken vehicle was lifted off the ground, being pulled back upright. Finally the balance of weight on the wheels was enough that the last two wheels smashed to the ground, uprighting it. Bruce rushed to the main door, knocking on it.

"Is everyone ok? Open up!" shouted Bruce.

The door swung open, and he went aboard. Aside from the minor injuries and one broken leg, they'd had a lucky escape. He went to the front of the vehicle where Jackson was beginning to wake up, still sitting in the driver's seat with his seat belt buckled. Bruce released the buckle of his belt and grabbed hold of his ear, forcing him to follow. He led the man out of the vehicle, revealing him to the two dozen people stood in front of them.

"This fuck muppet had the good sense to buckle his belt to save his own skin, and had no concern whatsoever for the rest of his crew, or any of us!" shouted Bruce.

He slammed the man against the side of the recently recovered vehicle, and punched him in the face, causing him to reel in pain, blood spurting from his nose.

"Ordinarily I would suggest some severe punishment for such blatant disregard for the group's safety. Sadly, we cannot spare one life, and that is the lesson that this idiot must learn. We may not all share the same interests, or be compatible people. Some of you may loathe others, but we are the lucky few, we can't be picky about who we call our friends anymore. Therefore, we're going to have to hope Jackson has learnt the errors of his ways, because nothing we can say will change him," said Bruce.

The group looked at each other, some mumbling, others agreeing. Many of the survivors had hoped to see some punishment dealt out to the man who had put them in such danger, they were in part disappointed, but also relieved that it was over.

"Jackson, wisen the fuck up, and don't you dare touch any alcohol for the rest of the week," said Bruce.

The bloodied and dazed man nodded, knowing he had no other choice. Bruce walked around to the side of the crashed vehicle to survey the damage, it was largely cosmetic. However, the mesh screens covering the windows were damaged and partly hanging off.

"Jake, organise some guys to get this fixed. Connor, we have wounded to attend to and vehicles to repair and check for damage, we hold here for the day, rest up and continue tomorrow!" shouted Bruce.

CHAPTER THREE

NORTHERN PACIFIC OCEAN

The Landing Craft Air Cushion (LCAC) bounced gently as it clipped the low waves of the ocean. The vehicle was an oddity, a shallow hulled but very wide landing craft that operated as a hovercraft. She travelled at forty knots and carried Captain Black's reconnaissance unit. Though the craft could carry half a dozen vehicles or even a couple of hundred soldiers there were far fewer onboard for this operation. Captain Black brought with him a well-equipped Marine platoon, as well as several specialists from the US and France that they had stuck with since their experiences in Afghanistan in the months before. There was also a number of civilian technical crew led by Dr Garcia.

Dr Garcia cradled her rugged laptop as she watched

the screen for useful information. The computer had a live feed to the UAV that buzzed overhead and provided the unit with up-to-date information on the ship and the immediate area around them. The display showed several access points near the bow that were used for loading materials directly into the hull. She turned to the Marines that were readying equipment and spotted the Captain. She waved to him, drawing his attention to the computer. He said a few more words and then wandered over, shouting over the sound of the loud fans.

"What?" he asked.

"Look!" shouted Dr Garcia as she showed him the access hatches.

Captain Black nodded in agreement and gave her a thumbs up gesture. He tapped his ear and then spoke into his throat mic, giving directions to the crew of the craft. They were now only half a mile from the bow of the massive ocean liner.

Overhead a helicopter buzzed past, it was the research vessel's own craft and carried an additional four Marines. Moving swiftly past the hovercraft it approached the liner and hovered over the bow of the vessel. Ropes appeared and in less than a minute the Marines had rappelled down to the deck and started fixing ropes to throw down to the hovercraft below. With the Marines safely disgorged it turned and flew back to the ship.

Sergeant Fernanda organised the small group as they

hurled the ropes over the port side of the vessel. She was a tough Marine and had been part of Captain Black's unit back in Afghanistan when they first encountered both the Taliban and the undead.

"Captain, ropes are in. We're securing the position, give us thirty seconds, out," she spoke on her hands free radio equipment.

With just a single hand signal the Marines spread out, examining the large front section of the super liner. The bow section was shaped like a large letter 'v' and was completely flat, save for the containers heaped onto the deck. The Sergeant moved to the port side of the vessel so she could see down the side of the ship. It all looked clear from her position.

"Port side is clear," she reported on her radio, 'waiting for the status of the starboard side."

From opposite she spotted Brent, one of the newest members of the unit, signalling the other side of the ship was clear.

"All clear, I repeat you are clear to board," she said firmly.

"Affirmative," came the response.

Sergeant Fernanda smiled to herself, recognising the coolness she always associated with Captain Black. He certainly didn't like to waste words. Overhead the UAV buzzed past, its small engine grumbling as it moved off towards the aft of the ship. Fernanda pulled out her military issue PDA and accessed the live feed the aircraft was transmitting. They had started using these smaller, unit operated UAVs in the urban combat whilst she was in Iraq and they provided a critical view when a unit's line of sight was blocked. As the craft continued she noted the missing life craft and boats, as well as what looked like red or black marks on the floor.

Brent arrived back whilst the other two helped the first of the Marines from the hovercraft up onto the deck.

"Brent, look at this," she said as she handed the device over to him.

"Hmm, it could be a spill of some kind, looks like dried blood though," he answered as he passed the device back.

"Yeah, knowing our luck it will definitely be blood," said Fernanda sarcastically.

More of the Marines pulled themselves up over the side of the ship and onto the forecastle. As each hit the deck they readied their weapons and spread out to provide cover if needed. Captain Black pulled himself over, assisted by another of the Marines and dropped onto the deck. He spotted the Sergeant and moved directly to her. As he approached she stood to attention and saluted him.

"Report, Sergeant," he ordered.

Sergeant Fernanda turned her PDA towards the Captain and showed him the latest data.

"So far the upper decks look clear though we have spotted signs of a struggle, especially in this area," she said as she hit the review button.

The display went backwards in time until it reached the point where the UAV had passed what looked like blood. Captain Black examined the feed in detail before making a call on his radio.

"Bring up the doctor," he turned to Sergeant Fernanda. "Good work, set up a temporary command post in the bridge, he pointed upwards to the large structure covered in thick glass windows.

"Leave the ropes in position in case we need to leave in a hurry. I want a three man detail guarding the forecastle. The rest will split into two teams and work their way up to the bridge. I'll take the port side, you take the starboard and we'll meet in the middle.

"Just like old times, Sir," replied Sergeant Fernanda with a smile.

She moved off to organise the rest of the Marines whilst Captain Black went back to his radio.

"Black here. We've secured the forecastle and are moving onto the bridge. Any updates on signs of survivors?" he asked.

There was a short pause before one of the crew from the Moreau called back.

"Captain Black, we have a very weak signal coming from the Grand Lobby."

"What kind of signal?" he asked as he checked his printed diagram of the ship.

The massive vessel contained over seventeen passenger decks and the Grand Lobby was just over a third the way along the ship and low down in the hull. It would take some time to work their way from the forecastle to reach it. The radio crackled.

"We are receiving a series of low frequency sounds. They are unlikely to be equipment as they're not in a continuous rhythm. There's a chance it's survivors."

"Yeah, also a chance of a hundred zombies in there trying to claw their way out," he muttered off the radio.

"Understood. Will reappraise the situation, once we control the bridge section of the ship."

"Good luck," came the reply.

Captain Black turned to the troops on the deck. They were already divided up into three groups, the smaller one stayed near the ropes on the port side. The other two groups consisted of a dozen Marines, each of them equipped with worn but functional digital camouflage and a selection of body armour and weapons. Unlike combat units of just a year ago there were some noticeable changes to their clothing since the outbreak. The first was that they all wore sturdy gloves with reinforced protection on the wrists. On the rest of their arms were what looked like lacrosse armour that ran from the forearm to the shoulder. The extra armoured sections were made of toughened cloth and plastic and were designed to protect against bites from the undead. On their legs they wore similar armour that ran from the shins to just above the knee. The final piece of unusual equipment was neck armour that looked like a padded ring around the throat, a piece of equipment often used in hockey to protect the windpipe. Though they were of no use against combat units these modifications had saved the Marines in scores of battles.

Each Marine carried a mixture of M16 rifles, M4 carbines, Heckler & Koch MP5 submachine guns and pistols. With supplies running low each Marine stuck with the weapon they had easy access to. This meant a few of them carried non-issue shotguns and weapons taken from the battlefield. Though this led to some irregularity with the firearms, it was hardly surprising in the circumstances.

"Listen up, we have information on possible survivors in the Grand Lobby section. We'll secure the bridge and attempt to activate the video feeds before moving deeper into the ship. Assume every section is contaminated and exercise extreme caution. I want a zero casualty rate on this one. Secure the stairs, doorways and access points; once the bridge is secure, nothing gets in. Understood?"

He was greeted by a chorus of "Ooh-rah".

"Let's go then!" he shouted.

Captain Black led the first dozen along the port side of the ship, each Marine staying close to the edge of the vessel and away from the superstructure. On the opposite side of the ship Sergeant Fernanda led her unit towards the access hatch that led inside the lower sections below the bridge. Upon her signal Corporal Kowalski moved to the hatch and attempted to open it. He was no weakling but the hatch refused to budge.

"Fuck! It's locked down Sarge, probably from the inside," he called.

"Blow it!" said Fernanda.

Corporal Armstrong moved up to the door and placed a small number of charges in place. It took just seconds to fit them to the key points on the hatch. With a hand signal he ordered the unit to pull back from the blast zone and when far enough away hit the button. With a dull crump the hatch blasted inside and exposed a space of approximately one metre wide, perfectly big enough for a Marine to enter. Kowalski went in first, quickly followed by Fernanda and the rest of the unit.

On the port side of the vessel Captain Black found the doorway to the secondary stairwell was unlocked and still open. He signalled to Gunnery Sergeant Freeman, a tough, well built Marine, to clear the entry point before they moved inside. The Marine moved to the entrance and pushed an electronic device inside the doorway. The device was a remote camera system and provided detailed thermal and visible light imaging of the area. He turned back to the Captain.

"It looks clear to me, no sign of life or movement anywhere in there," he said.

Black gave the signal and the rest of the group moved into the stairwell, each of the Marines scanned around to make sure no surprises would impede their progress. The Marines were all equipped with lanterns either fixed to their shoulders or to their weapons. The beams provided a dull yellow glow to the dark and dusty interior.

With the deck level secured the Marines moved up the staircase and continued on their mission to the bridge. Some of the emergency lights provided a small amount of red lighting, but most of the route was dark and unlit.

On the starboard side of the vessel Fernanda and her unit were already up two floors when they came across the first bodies. On the floor were several corpses, as well as three twisted and contorted bodies that were obviously zombies. The main difference was that the clothing of the zombies was torn and damaged as well as their skin and flesh. The zombie bodies were also damaged, with at least one missing a limb. The other bodies were unharmed, apart from a small number of bite wounds and injuries. The Marines had experienced these kinds of bodies before and were all too familiar with the dangers.

The Marines placed a remote sensor unit that combined thermal imaging and a rotating camera unit that could monitor the entire floor. Continuing past the bodies they moved up the stairwell and to the part of the ship known as the Commodore's Club. This was a small but exclusive bar that provided views out over the bow of the ship. The door leading inside was half open and a body in a uniform was sprawled out blocking the way in.

Fernanda updated Captain Black with her progress.

"Sir, we have secured the floor leading to the Commodore's Bar. We'll clear this section then meet you at the bridge," she said.

"Understood, we are one floor above you and approaching the luxury suites. Be careful, we've found bodies from the crew and the undead already," answered Captain Black.

Sergeant Fernanda entered the bar, closely followed by three more Marines who raised their weapons, scanning for signs of trouble. The bar was smaller than she expected but it was well furnished. All along the length of the room were windows facing forwards. She moved up and spotted the Marines out in the forecastle. To the left was a small group in civilian attire, which must have been Dr Garcia and her assistants.

"Sir, it looks like the Doctor has arrived on the forecastle," she said into her radio.

"Affirmative," came the response.

Looking around she was satisfied the room was clear.

"Close it up, we need to keep moving."

They left the room whilst they sealed it securely behind them and then returned to the stairwell. Moving upwards they entered a small lobby area that led to the luxury suites. These were the forward facing accommodation and therefore the most expensive and prestigious parts of the ship to stay in. All of the doors were either broken open or slightly ajar.

Throughout the open area a number of bodies were dotted around, as well as blood stains and burn marks. It was a main hub for this part of the ship and the number of bodies suggested quite a few people had been caught out there.

Johnson examined part of the damaged wall and then double-checked two of the bodies. He turned to Sergeant Fernanda.

"There was definitely a battle of some kind here, look," he said as he pointed to a number of objects near the bodies.

As she stepped forwards Johnson prised what looked like an improvised maul from the fingers of the dead man on the floor.

"Yeah, I've seen this before. Be careful," she said.

The communication system clicked, informing her that Captain Black was approaching the luxury suites from the other side.

"Hold your fire, friendlies coming in from there," she pointed to the doorway leading to the port stairwell.

The door opened and two Marines each one carrying an M4 carbine entered, both of them looking for signs of the enemy. Sergeant Fernanda gave them a thumbs up signal which they then passed on to those waiting on the staircase. They moved up to Fernanda, Captain Black came up next and the rest followed. The unit was now reassembled in the open area at the luxury suites.

"According to my plans the bridge is directly above us," said Captain Black. "You, you and you, check the rooms."

The three men moved off to examine the suites whilst Captain Black and Sergeant Fernanda discussed the next move.

"This area leads off in three directions and it's a critical hub for this part of the ship. It is essential that we maintain control of this. I don't want us trapped in the bridge with no way to get out. I want you and your Marines to cover the open lobby here, the corridor leading to both stairwells. We'll proceed to the bridge, I'll update you when we get there."

"Understood. Do you think you'll be able to get the security systems online?" she asked.

"I doubt it. This ship is state of the art and according to Dr Garcia, contains the latest networked security systems. Why do you think she's coming aboard?"

"Let's hope she can get the system online then."

Captain Black nodded and then headed for the stairwell.

"First Squad with me, Second Squad stay with Sergeant Fernanda," he ordered.

Without pausing the Captain left the open area and started working his way up the staircase, the rest of his squad followed. Sergeant Fernanda then turned to her own squad and organised her Marines into defensive positions. Their first job was to cover each key point, but once these were secured they then pulled out furniture from the suites to form a series of rudimentary barricades. In less than three minutes the lobby had been turned into a small fort with cover facing the corridor, suites and entrances to both stairwells. With that kind of cover the dozen Marines should have no trouble defending the area.

With half of the squad in the centre guarding the lobby the rest split into three groups of two so that they could patrol the immediate area for intruders. After facing many similar situations though, none of them ventured so far as to be out of sight of the rest of the group.

Captain Black was the first to reach the entrance to the bridge. Like most of the rest of the ship the doors were ajar, but unlike previous locations there were no bodies to be seen. He entered the section and moved inside. All along the one side were a dozen screens. There were a substantial number of windows providing an excellent view of the forecastle, bow and both sides of the ship. In front of the computer screens were lots of chairs, each of them facing the displays and the windows. The Captain moved to what looked like the most important position and pressed a few keys on the system. Though there were a few lights on, none of the computers appeared to turn on and the screens remained dark and lifeless.

"Dr Garcia, the forward section of the ship is secured.

We could do with you and your technicians to get this ship active. What is your ETA?" he spoke into his radio.

There was a short pause before the familiar voice of the Doctor replied.

"Captain Black, we are in the stairwell and on our way up, I estimate two minutes before we arrive. Please don't touch anything till we get there," she said in a serious tone.

One of the Marines dumped a large pack onto the floor in the middle of the bridge and proceeded to unload various communications and surveillance equipment. The first item out was a rugged looking laptop. He placed it on top of the first box and flicked the switch. As it started up a serious of small windows popped up, each showing a view from the cameras the Marines has set up so far. He then flipped out a secondary screen from the rear of the machine that showed another two views, one from the UAV and the other from the hovercraft that was returning to the ships.

The door opened and in walked Dr Garcia, flanked by two of her personal security guards. These men were very well armed and wearing purpose built body armour, perfectly designed for use in infected areas. She walked onto the bridge and looked around, taking in the computer terminals, networked systems and power units dotted about. She then turned to Captain Black.

"This is as expected. The equipment looks undamaged but we don't have the main power back up do we?" she asked.

"That's correct, from my plans we would need to reach the auxiliary engine room to reactivate the power."

"That's ok. We aren't looking at taking the ship. We just need enough power to get the computer system and network back up so we can see what's going on here," she replied.

Two more Marines arrived. They were carrying Dr Garcia's equipment and placed it down near their own surveillance equipment. Dr Garcia gave their gear a quick glance.

"Quaint," she said annoyingly and then turned to her own people.

"Get the portable power rigs up. You, set up my system over there next to the network switches," she ordered.

The Marine nodded and started moving the equipment to the appropriate place. Captain Black moved up to the Doctor.

"Nice to see you're getting comfortable here. How long do you need to get the security feeds back up?" he asked.

"Well, I anticipate it will take around fifteen minutes to power up the bridge's systems and then up to ten minutes to break the security. I've checked the system specifications and it shouldn't be too much of a problem…assuming no more interruptions," she said.

"Then don't waste time talking to me," he said as he moved back to the group of Marines waiting at the other side of the bridge. As he made his way across the room he radioed in.

"Black here. Bridge is secure, suites secure and forecastle is secure. Anticipate access to security feeds in approximately twenty five minutes," he reported.

"Affirmative. Do you require anything else for your operation?" came the reply from Captain Mathius back onboard the ship.

"Negative, we have everything we need. Just make sure the helo and LCAC are ready in case we hit trouble. We don't know what else is out here," answered Captain Black.

"Understood."

The lights in the room flickered, causing Captain Black to look back at Dr Garcia and her team. One of the technicians looked back at him, noting his interest.

"We're getting there," he said, almost apologetically.

* * *

Sergeant Fernanda and her squad were secure in their position outside the luxury suites, just one level below the bridge. In the fifteen minutes since they'd been there they'd come across no movement, either dead or alive. On the improvised barricade one of the Marines had set up his M249 machine gun and was scanning it from side to side, looking for trouble down the dark hallways.

Fernanda's radio crackled.

"This is Black, we have partial feeds up and working. I'm sending down six men to relieve you."

"Sir?" replied Fernanda.

"I need you to take your squad directly to the Grand Lobby and fast."

"Have you found something?" she asked, sounding concerned.

"Most of the cameras are down in the aft section of the ship and a large number are also down near the Grand Lobby. We've managed to isolate sounds in that area though and it seems there's movement there, but we cannot determine whether it's survivors or the undead. We have a route that appears clear to get you there."

"What's the rush? Can't we wait until we have more intel before we go in?" she said.

"We could, but it seems the ship has problems, serious problems."

"What do you mean?" asked Fernanda.

As she waited for a reply she signalled to the Marines patrolling the corridor leading to the aft of the vessel.

"This is Dr Garcia here. I've gained access to engineering and it seems there are problems with the refrigeration plant's engines. They are positioned deep in the centre of the vessel, at the bottom near the bilge. From the information I have it seems there are major electrical failures in that area and increases in heat," she said.

"A fire?" asked Fernanda.

"Yes. Either the electrical system has failed and started a series of fires, or more likely there are survivors who in their struggles they have either accidentally or deliberately set these sections on fire," she replied.

The voice on the radio changed abruptly as Captain Black took over.

"Either way, Sergeant, you need to get your team aft and fast. I'm sending the Doctor's route to your PDA now," he said.

As their conversation continued the port stairwell door opened to reveal the relief unit of Marines that had been sent down by the Captain. Fernanda called out to her unit.

"Listen up!" she barked whilst she grabbed her M4 carbine.

The Marines moved back to her as she explained the plan whilst she slung the weapon across her torso. Without stopping she pulled on her armoured lower arm guard and moved off down the corridor and into the darkness of the ship.

* * *

Captain Black and Dr Garcia watched the numerous displays on the equipment they had both brought. Whilst the Marines' equipment provided video feeds from the Marines themselves, Dr Garcia's equipment and her work with the ship's system provided limited viewpoints of different parts of the ship. It wasn't perfect but it was a lot better than no footage. On the one screen they could see the entire length of a long corridor. It led from their original starting position towards the rear of the ship. The Marines had already travelled about a hundred metres along it when they appeared on the cameras. One of the technicians hit a few keys and managed to get several of the lights to come on, providing some illumination for the small unit of Marines.

One of the smaller screens showed a feed coming directly from Corporal Armstrong. He'd taken point for the unit as they made their slow progress through the ship.

A light started flashing on one of the computers followed by a low toned alarm.

"What's that?" asked Captain Black.

"It's detected movement on one of the ship's cameras. I've modified the protocols here to detect image pattern changes rather than heat changes," answered Dr Garcia.

The Marine officer nodded, immediately understanding the point of the changes.

"Yeah, that makes sense. Passive infrared is useless against the dead as they're as cold as the walls of the ship. Can we see what is causing the movement?" he asked.

Dr Garcia gave him a glance, pleasantly surprised at the knowledge of a mere Marine, before turning back to the screen.

"Let's see what I can do," she said whilst making a few

tweaks.

The screen flashed and then revealed a dark, very noisy image with what looked like a large moving silhouette.

"Fuck!" swore Captain Black as he grabbed for the radio mic.

"Fernanda, you've got hostiles moving in about four rooms down on the left," he shouted.

"Affirmative," she replied.

Another light flashed on a different display showing similar movement in one of the function rooms off to the right of the Marines' position. Before they could pass on the information the camera picked up the door being torn open and a dozen shapes staggered out into the hallway.

"Sergeant!" shouted Captain Black.

The screens on the Marines' equipment flickered as they tried to adjust to the light changes as they opened fire. The one CCTV camera in the corridor showed a mass of people and muzzle flashes.

Captain Black moved for the door but Dr Garcia grabbed at him.

"There's nothing you can do for them by running off. They know what they're doing. I need you and your men's help to get more of the systems online so we can get them to the Grand Lobby in time," she said.

Captain Black looked back at the screen to see the flashes had stopped and the Marines were still moving along the corridor. With a crackle Sergeant Fernanda's voice returned.

"That was fun. We were jumped by two groups of them, no casualties to report. We are continuing on," she said.

"Good work, Sergeant. We have a clear route coming up shortly, keep your eyes peeled."

There was a short delay before Fernanda replied.

"Understood, Captain."

* * *

Kowalski and Armstrong moved to the end of the corridor and into the open space leading to the stairwells and main elevator system. The rest of the Marines took up positions to cover the access to the stairwells. Sergeant Fernanda called back to the bridge.

"We're at the entrance to the stairwells, do you have any intel on them?" she asked.

"We have movement from the level immediately above the Grand Lobby, everything above that looks clear. Don't take any chances though," answered the Captain.

"Affirmative," replied Fernanda.

She gave a signal to Armstrong who slowly opened the door and shone his torch inside. He turned back and waved them to follow. He moved in and rushed down as quickly as he dared, the rest of the unit close behind. In a matter of thirty seconds the Marines were positioned above the Grand Lobby. The stairs had already transformed into a beautiful spiral grand staircase and the furnishing matched in details and quality. Kowalski leaned over towards Armstrong.

"Holy shit, now this I like," he whispered.

"Yeah," replied the Marine, "rather be back on our own boat though."

"Amen to that," whispered Jackson, who was waiting patiently in the darkness with his Heckler and Koch MP5 lifted and ready for action.

"We're in position," whispered Fernanda into her mic.

"We have you on the screen. From here onwards the security system is inactive. We have no idea what you will find. I repeat. You are entering an unknown, potentially hostile area. Take it easy and if you hit trouble, fall back towards the theatre," answered Captain Black.

"Also, be careful, you are directly above the refrigeration plants and that's where we think the problems are concentrated," added Dr Garcia.

"Understood, we're going in," said Sergeant Fernanda as she gave the signal.

Kowalski and Armstrong entered the grand staircase first, with the rest of the Marines spaced out in a long column behind them. They inched their way down, using their lights on the lowest settings to avoid drawing too much attention. As Armstrong rounded the first bend he looked over the ledge and down into the exquisite lobby below. Surprisingly some of the lights were still working and provided light to the more enclosed areas. The staircase led to a wide open gallery in a semi-circle shape. At the centre of the semi-circle was a rounded glass platform that split off into two spiralling staircases, both had thick red carpet.

"Nice," whispered Kowalski.

The Marines continued towards the glass platform that offered a complete view of the lobby area.

"Fernanda here. We're in the lobby area, top of the main staircases on the platform," she said.

"Got you. Take the left staircase, follow it around to the left and past the pianos. That's where the source of the sound is."

"Affirmative," answer Fernanda.

With a signal to fan out the Marines moved down the staircase and spread out along the base, each of them scanning the wide open lobby for signs of movement. Though some of the lights lit the corners there were still sections that were too dark to make out. A sound came from below, as though somebody had kicked a box or crate over. The Sergeant clenched her fist and raised it up, the rest of the Marines halted and dropped to the ground, expecting trouble.

"Hey, Sarge," whispered Private Hopkins, "take a look at this."

The Marine was pointing across the lobby to a flickering

light. Fernanda crept over to him whilst the rest of them held steady. She looked carefully, her eyes adjusting to the lighting in the room. She reached down to her pocket and pulled out a small military issue camera and held it up to her eye. It was a combined low light and thermal imaging camera. In the screen the area of the flickering light was showing as extremely hot. She panned the camera, examining the rest of the lobby until she spotted movement. She panned back and spotted more of the hot areas.

There was a flash from the end of the lobby and a series of flames licked up towards the other side of the staircase. Another dull rumble echoed through the ship.

"Fuck, sounds like something serious is going on down there," said Weston, the squad's M249 machine gunner, as he pointed at the floor.

The ground shuddered from what felt like several blasts, possibly explosions. Sergeant Fernanda lost her foot and stumbled, managing to catch one of the columns at the last moment. She called on her radio.

"Captain, I've got people down here, a group of about a dozen are hiding inside one of the small function rooms. It also looks like we have a series of fires here. At least two in the lobby and the entire floor is showing as warming on my camera," she said.

She looked around the lobby, noting the flames that seemed to be growing fast. On her camera the heat seemed to be spreading through more sections of the ship. Her headset crackled.

"Good work. Be careful, Sergeant, if they're hiding it's for a reason. According to our data the refrigeration section is burning and burning hot. At this rate the vessel is going to start taking on water in the lower section of the hull sometime in the next three hours. You don't want to be there for too long. This is a death ship in more ways than one."

"Understood, heading to them now," she replied.

She moved off the staircase and around the columns in the direction of the small function rooms that ran along the one wall of the lobby. She signalled to the men to spread out into two groups, one each side of the area. As they moved a series of loud noises came from the function room.

Fernanda moved up to the door and placed her hand on the centre, it was cool to the touch. She turned back to ensure the rest of the Marines were with her before pushing it open and moving inside. On the floor there were pieces of splintered wood and a large wooden unit was pushed aside. Fernanda new instantly what had happened there, the survivors had nailed the door shut and then moved these items up against it to stop the creatures from getting inside.

She stepped to the right and in a matter of seconds the first six Marines were inside and pointing their weapons at the sight ahead of them. The room was packed with dozens of the undead and they were all hammering at a series of obstructions that were obviously an attempt at some kind of fortification. In the corner of the room the glint of an axe or something similar caught her attention. She turned to her squad.

"Watch for friendlies, clear the room!" she shouted.

Armstrong opened up first, quickly followed by a series of rifles. The streaks from the weapons blasted across the room, ripping into the undead throwing blood and guts on the walls. As soon as the weapons started another door opened to the side revealing another large horde of the creatures. The first three were close to the squad's machine gunner who cut them down with a long burst from his M249. The box magazine provided him with a hundred rounds of 5.56mm bullets and this firepower decimated the ambush.

Private Hopkins rushed forwards to the survivors and shouted over to them.

"Keep your heads down, we're here to help you!" he cried.

He pulled at the barricade, trying to reach them before another group of zombies moved from behind the debris against the wall. The first grabbed his leg whilst another pushed into his stomach, forcing him to the floor. A third dropped down to bite him only to be stopped by the muzzle of Fernanda's M4 carbine. A short burst sent the zombie's skull and brain up against the wall. Kowalski ran over and grabbed the second zombie off him and smashed his weapon into its face. He followed his attack up with another two rounds, one to the head and another to the torso. The rest of the unit spread out firing into the horde and cutting them down in just ten seconds of shooting.

Once the firing stopped Fernanda stepped up to the barricade, looking for the survivors.

"I am Sergeant Fernanda of the United States Marine Corps. You're safe now," she said.

From behind the barricade a young man stood up, quickly followed by more people. The man wore a torn and battered official uniform, presumably one of the crew. He climbed over the debris and down to the Marines. More followed, helped by the Marines.

"Can you help us with the wounded?" asked the man.

Fernanda signalled to her men who moved over to assist.

"How many of you are there?" she asked.

"Seven crew including me plus a dozen passengers," he replied.

"That's it, from the entire ship?"

He stepped up to the Sergeant.

"Yes," he replied, looking a little confused before holding out his hand.

"I'm sorry. I'm Carter, Sam Carter. I'm Head of

Security here. We're all that's left, thank God you came!" he said in a relieved tone.

As he moved forward a rumble came from deep in the ship followed by a series of low thumps underfoot. One of the paintings tipped and then fell from the wall, whilst chunks of plaster cracked and dropped from the ceiling.

"How long has it been like this?" asked Fernanda.

"For the last two days. We've been on the run since they overran the ship. There were over a hundred of us on the deck waiting for the boats when they hit us. A rescue unit was trying to hold them back when they triggered some explosions near the engine room," he said.

He turned and helped one of the children over the debris and into the open before continuing.

"We've been barricaded in here ever since and the fires have been spreading. We kept holding the creatures back, but we lost people every time. I don't think we could have managed more than a few days more."

Fernanda's radio crackled into life.

"Sergeant, we've got a big problem here. Get your people off the ship and fast," ordered Captain Black.

"What's going on?" she asked.

"Two things. Problem number one is your firefight has drawn attention. We're picking up movement on seven decks heading your way. They're in their hundreds, maybe thousands."

"Fuck! And the second?" she asked.

"The fires are spreading through the hull so fast we calculate the entire length of the ship will be burning in less than fifteen minutes. If you don't get topside fast you could be trapped."

"Understood, we're out of here," she answered quickly before turning to her unit.

"Marines, we need to go, come on!" she shouted as she left the room, closely followed by the mixture of survivors and soldiers.

* * *

Captain Black stared at the computer screen intently, watching the return route of Fernanda's unit. Half of the cameras were now down due to the electrical damage caused by the fires. Dr Garcia was typing away on one of the computers, whilst issuing orders to her own staff on the ship.

"Doctor, do you have what you need?" he asked.

"We've managed to collect medical supplies, fuel and some food from the lower storage areas and crew compartments. My people are loading everything onto the LCAC, they will be finished in about ten minutes," she answered.

Some quiet gunshots came from within the ship. Captain Black looked down at the screen, spotting movement the floor below where the Marines had set up the defensive position. The monitor flashed each time a weapon was discharged.

"Sir, we've got company here. Multiple targets, shit, Sir!" came the voice on the radio.

A dull thump indicated the use of a grenade followed by more rapid fire, presumably that of automatic weapons and machine-guns. Captain Black turned to Dr Garcia only to find her and her two guards already packing up her gear. He spoke into his microphone.

"Hold steady, son, we're coming for you," he said.

He grabbed his carbine and moved for the door. Dr Garcia reached out, trying to stop him.

"We need to get the rest of the supplies off the ship!" she ordered.

"No, you need to. My men will be on the forecastle in five minutes. Be there or get left behind," he barked and he stormed out.

In the distance the gunfire was louder and the sound of machine-gun fire increased. Dr Garcia looked at her two guards, one of them shrugged then cocked his weapon.

"Come on, follow him," she said.

* * *

Inside the ship Fernanda's group made their way towards the front of the vessel. Having moved out from the Grand Lobby they had already passed through the planetarium and were almost halfway back when they found the container. It was about fifteen feet long and big enough to park a medium sized truck inside.

Armstrong moved to the back of the container, noticing one part was open. He looked inside, moving his torch first one way then back again.

"Uh, Sarge, you need to take a look at this!" he shouted.

Fernanda moved towards him, but signalled for the rest of the group to keep moving. Once she reached the container she peered around the corner to look at whatever Armstrong had found. Inside were several shelves, each with a series of metallic cases, one portable computer and lots of blood.

"Holy shit. What is this?" she said.

"No idea, I bet the doc would want some of it though," he replied.

"Yeah, good idea. Bag what you can then follow us. We need to keep moving."

An explosion rocked the ship, sending some of the Marines hard against the walls of the corridor. Kowalski hit a pillar hard, stunning him and knocking him to the ground. One of the doors twisted and then fell down sending a fireball streaming to the group. Two of the Marines took the full force of the blast, their clothing and equipment catching alight and sending them screaming to the ground. Another blast shook ahead as part of the ceiling collapsed, blocking their route.

Fernanda lifted herself up, wiping the dust from her face as she surveyed the scene. The two Marines were down, their smouldering bodies needed no checking. The rest of the unit was coming back to their senses when she spotted movement off into the distance, it was the horde.

"Come on, we need to take the staircase, follow me!" she shouted.

She turned back towards the container and tore open the doorway that led to the staircase. Apart from the smoke and dust it appeared clear. She moved inside first and started making her way up the stairs, the rest of the group staggered behind her.

"Captain Black, are you receiving, over," she called on the radio.

A voice came back but it was hard to hear, it sounded like a broken voice, punctuated by noise. It went silent then the voice came back.

"Sergeant, good to hear your voice. We're under attack near the bridge!" he shouted.

The audio crackled from the sound of small arms fire in the background. There was shouting and screams before the calmer voice of the Captain came back.

"We're evacuating the area, falling back to the forecastle. Can you make it there?" he asked.

Three zombies appeared on the staircase, staggering towards her. She lifted her carbine and pulled the trigger. The weapon clicked but jammed. Without hesitating she withdrew her Beretta M9 9mm pistol and emptied six rounds into them. The first two were knocked down but the third kept on coming. Armstrong pushed past her and emptied a dozen rounds from head to toe into the last zombie. The rest of the group chased behind, desperate to reach the higher decks.

Another blast came from much closer, followed by the entire ceiling collapsing just twenty feet away.

"Move it!" shouted Fernanda as she pushed the Marines on past her.

As they went past another door a chink of light appeared, presumably from one of the upper decks.

One of the Marines booted it open, letting in fresh air and bright light. They staggered into the open as more blasts shook the vessel.

* * *

Captain Black and his surviving three Marines worked their way aft, on their way to Fernanda. Dr Garcia was close behind, flanked by her two guards. Her personal communication system beeped, informing her that the rest of her staff had evacuated the forecastle. About twenty feet behind them a massive horde gave chase, held back only by their slow movement.

"Black here, what is your status?" he called on his radio.

"We're topside and heading to you," Fernanda replied.

"Evac is on the way, meet at the landing pad forward of the first funnel," said Captain Black.

More creatures appeared in front of them, blocking their route to the top deck. Black lifted his carbine and emptied an entire magazine into the beasts. More zombies clambered over the bodies, making their way towards them. A series of blasts shook the corridor as the Marines attempted to hold back the horde.

Part of the false wall to the side of Garcia ripped apart and two zombies fell out, one knocking her to the floor.

"Fuck!" she shouted as she hit the ground.

"Doctor!" shouted one of the guards and he rushed forwards to help, followed by the second guard.

More fire poured from the Marines who did their best to stem the tide. Dr Garcia lifted her Heckler & Koch MP7 from her thigh holster and shredded the first zombie with a long burst of automatic fire. One of her guards slammed his armoured fist into the second whilst another zombie climbed out and bit down into his shoulder. Luckily the reinforced armour protected him from the strong bite long enough for his comrade to empty several rounds into the creature's face.

Sergeant Black helped her up and they kept moving forwards, firing at the following undead. He kicked open the door leading to the upper deck and led the survivors out into the open. He ran down the staircase leading to the port side landing pad. It took almost a full minute for them all to reach it. As they stepped down onto the ship's main deck they spotted Fernanda's group heading right towards them. A dark crowd of the undead was behind them. The pad was only fifty feet away.

Off to his right Captain Black spotted the LCAC drifting away from the ship, it looked loaded down with crates, supplies and people. From its loading bay tracer arced, they were presumably fighting off their own problems.

"Captain Mathius, where is that evac?" he called into his radio.

With a deafening roar two Bell UH-1Y Venom Super Huey's swept past the ship, heavy weapons' fire coming from their door mounted machineguns.

"Holy shit, that's good timing," said one of the Doctor's guards.

"Come on!" shouted Black, as he moved to the landing pad.

From the lower deck doors more zombies staggered out, all of them heading for the noise of the first helicopter as it descended to the pad. With the pads so low on the vessel they were only just big enough for one aircraft at a time. As Captain Black arrived at the edge of the pad he spotted the rescued civilians packing into the helicopter, Fernanda had beaten them to it. Lifting his weapon he fired another dozen rounds at the zombies. Turning back he helped Dr Garcia and the rest of his people whilst one of the Marines provided covering fire.

Sergeant Fernanda rushed over, tapping him on the shoulder. Before she could speak, the first Huey lifted off, making space for the second aircraft.

"You made it!" she shouted.

"You bet!" he replied. "Can we all fit on the next chopper?" he asked.

She turned back, counting the number of people in her head.

"No way, three of us are going to have to stay behind!"

As the second Super Huey landed he started to strip off his body armour and gear.

"How did your water training go, Sergeant?" he asked with a grin.

Fernanda grinned as she pulled at the Velcro straps on her webbing.

Armstrong appeared, helping Dr Garcia to the aircraft whilst the rest of the unit piled into the helicopter.

"Come on you two, we need to go!" said the Captain.

Armstrong turned back and was helped into the overcrowded aircraft. Captain Black waved them off, shouting into his headset to go. The zombies were now at the pad and lifting themselves up. The Captain pulled out his handgun and emptied the weapon at the first to climb the ledge.

The pilot, obviously shaken by the appearance of the zombies applied power and the aircraft started to lift off, leaving Captain Black, Fernanda and Kowalski. More of the zombies climbed onto the pad and started moving towards their little group.

"Time to go!" laughed Fernanda as she ran for the edge and leapt off the vessel and towards the deep ocean.

CHAPTER FOUR

ENGLAND

Dave was peering out of the window as the Land Rover chugged on down the wet and muddy country road. He was armoured up in an assortment of anything that would provide protection. A battered old biker's jacket was the base layer on his body, with a custom built armoured vest on top. The last year had taught him that he didn't have to just protect himself from the zombies, but hostile humans too. This metal plate lined armour provided sturdy protection from a shotgun shell or hand-to-hand weapon. Around his legs he wore thick leather armour, re-enforced with metal splints.

Beside Dave sat Tommy, his closest friend over the last few months. Tommy was an aggressive man who would always jump in at the deep end, but was also a worthy ally.

At twenty four years old when the outbreak begun, he'd worked in a factory assembling cars.

The old hunk of iron that carried them was a series Land Rover, older than either of the men in it. The 109-inch wheelbase truck that they lovingly referred to as Kate after their favourite movie star, was retro fitted with armour plating and chicken wire.

"That was a shit haul," said Tommy.

"True, but it'll help," said Dave.

"It's not enough though, is it?" said Tommy.

He was referring to their most recent haul. They'd been on a raid to find supplies, them and the other vehicle behind them. The second vehicle, a Daihatsu Fourtrak, also had two occupants. The large quantities of red diesel held on the surrounding farms had given them a great head start on keeping their vehicles running. Two vehicles with two men each was the group's standard operating procedure, never risking too many people outside their compound, but always having a backup vehicle.

They arrived at large gates built from a mix of wood and metal parts bolted and welded together, with multiple layers of chicken wire spanning them entirely. The gates were eight feet high, the same as the walls they were attached to. This was the entrance to the place that Dave and many other survivors now called their home.

In reality, the compound was nothing more than a wealthy landowner's property that had been re-enforced with the help of survivors. The owner still lived in the house and commanded the ragtag group of survivors which had made it this far. The land spanned a hundred acres or more, but they controlled and commanded just ten.

The gates were pulled back by the man and woman who were on guard at that time and let the vehicles pass through. Dave gave a nod to Ben and Vicky who were on watch. They drove along the farm track to the house. It was a large old building, with six bedrooms, all now converted for them to live in. The lower windows of the house were still heavily barricaded from by initial defences from nearly a year before.

This compound housed just nineteen of the lucky few who had made it this far. Nobody truly knew how many humans were left in the world. Occasionally they met friendly survivors who would either stay a while and move on or occasionally make the place their home. More often than not the survivors they met were hostile.

Dave could never understand the number of people who turned on each other at such a time of crisis and need. Why, when so few humans inhabited the earth, would they choose to fight each other? Working together their odds of survival in both resources and combat were hugely improved, though not everyone understood that.

The vehicles pulled up in front of the old house. Roger, the man in charge and owner, was already walking out to greet them. The house was called Everglade, a name all now used to describe their home.

"How'd it go?" asked Roger.

"Not great," said Tommy.

"Didn't you find anything?" asked Roger.

"Yeah, sure. We found some stuff, he's just being a miserable bastard," said Dave.

"Fuck you!" said Tommy.

"Well come on then, let's see what you've got," said Roger.

Dave opened up the back of the Land Rover. They had foraged for supplies at a petrol station on the edge of a small town. Their leader would never let them roam into areas that used to be inhabited by large numbers of people. He deemed it far too risky. Not all the party agreed with this, but the command had been followed until this point. They had recovered various junk foods, crisps, chocolate bars, soft drinks and some alcohol.

"No canned food?" asked Roger.

"Unfortunately not," said Dave.

"Ah well, at least we can keep our sugar levels high!" said Roger.

The quirky landowner was ever the optimist. He was in his early sixties and had never really had to work much, having been born into money. Sadly, this luxury meant that he owned no livestock, nor knew anything of farming, other than how to keep the place looking tidy.

"We need to go where the good stuff is," said Tommy.

"We've been through this before, laddie. We go where it is relatively safe and nothing more," said Roger.

"But there are massive shops full of stuff waiting for us, we just have to go and get it," said Tommy.

"We're just a handful of survivors in a world that wants to eat us, we cannot afford just one life lost," said Roger.

"Then we do it quickly," said Tommy.

"I'm sorry, but I will not hear anymore of this, you must accept that we're doing what is best for all of us," said Roger.

"Come on, Tommy. We've been through this before," said Dave.

Tommy huffed in frustration, knowing this was a battle he couldn't win. He knew that he could bring back the best food any of them had seen since this began, but his superiors held him back. The hierarchy in this compound was a tricky thing. In part, your authority was dictated by how long you'd been there, Dave being one of the first handful and who commanded respect. Dave had never wanted power, but he'd settled well into being one of Roger's key men.

Roger had allocated ranks or positions to everyone in the group. His closest allies were known as Captains, which were Dave and one other, Luke. Roger considered combat training a priority, with everyone practicing regularly, though more recently he had begun to emphasise the need for self sufficiency. He'd almost lost two survivors in a raid that strayed too far into a town just a month before. He knew all too well that the food they could find in shops would only last a couple of years more, and that the real solution came in making or growing your own.

Dave noticed Kailey walking out of the house towards them, an ever growing smile stretching across her face. The very knowledge that he could see and talk to her each and every day was willpower enough to keep going. A reason to work at living was never something any of the survivors were used to, the protection of society was provided for them. Now, each and every one of them had to be determined to live.

"Good trip?" asked Kailey.

"As good as can be expected," said Dave.

"You ready to eat?" asked Kailey.

"Fucking right," said Tommy.

The group assembled inside the house for a meal. Roger had insisted from the moment the compound was secure, that they always sit down for a meal each evening. He said it was important to hold onto what little they had left of society and normal living. He was right, every man and woman in the group looked forward to the communal gatherings. Roger organised it so that five people were always on watch at any one time, meaning fourteen, at current population, could enjoy the meal together.

Food wasn't what it used to be. Fresh food had gone

off just days after the Zompoc started. Meals now consisted largely of canned food. But junk food played a large part of their daily intake of calories, as it at least stayed edible for years. They could procure more supplies of decent canned food, but it would mean much more risky operations into population centres.

The one thing that was never in short supply was alcohol, as it never really went off. Roger saw alcohol as an important element of morale within the compound, but he always restricted every individual's intake per day. Having your diet controlled was not always popular, but it insured everyone got what they needed and had nothing to excess. There was no place for obesity and drunkenness in this world anymore.

After the meal, Dave and Tommy headed up to bed, their missions to procure supplies counted as their watch time, so they rarely carried out guard duty. Guarding anything was boring, but most of the survivors were more than happy to stay within the safe confines of their home than risk their necks in the wilderness.

Being so far from any population centre the compound only ever saw the occasional zombie. Everglade had its own zombie pest control squad, five men who acted as a clean up squad. With the sparse population locally the squad could outnumber the creatures in combat, allowing them to fight in relative safety.

The two men lay down on the mattresses that were laid

out across the floor, a luxury in the world they now lived.

"You know what I wouldn't give for a can of corned beef, or tuna?" said Tommy.

"I'm with you there," said Dave.

"Then why don't we go get some?" asked Tommy.

"You know why," said Dave.

"Fuck that, we could get in and out safely," said Tommy.

"You don't know that, we cannot risk the lives of a single person," said Dave.

"But what about that supermarket, it's what, fifty miles from here, waiting to be plucked," said Tommy.

"Yes and it's attached to a town that had, and likely still has, a population of tens of thousands," said Dave.

"We can't go on eating nothing but shit," said Tommy.

"And we won't, you know Roger is already well into setting up the farming here, next year we'll have some good food of our own," said Dave.

"But that's a year, assuming he even knows what the fuck he's doing," said Tommy."

"I've heard enough, we aren't going anywhere near that town!" shouted Dave.

Tommy fell silent as both men finally began to relax, neither happy with each other's standpoint. Five men shared the room that they now used. Despite the house having so many bedrooms, many had to be used for storing supplies such as food, weapons, protective gear and other essential equipment.

Dave had been for the first time since the outbreak beginning to feel that things were starting to go his way. He'd managed to settle into a survivable location with decent people and some resemblance of a future. He forgot all about Tommy's grumblings and turned his mind simply to all the good things. Dave fell asleep, a welcome rest after the day's driving and work.

Dave was harshly awoken by Graham, the driver from one of the other vehicles the group used, it was 7.30am. He was barely awake but the adrenaline was quickly bringing him to an alert state. The zombie infested world had taught all of them that laziness and slack living was a death-trap.

"Dave, Dave, wake up!" shouted Graham.

Graham was nearly sixty years old. He'd arrived at the compound with his Land Rover Discovery a month after the outbreak, everyone was surprised he'd survived alone all that time. Graham was a widower used to living alone, and a highly practical man, if not a true fighter.

"What is it?" asked Dave.

"Tommy and three others have taken Kate and the Fourtrak driven off," said Graham.

"Where did they go?" asked Dave.

"No idea, Kyle and Amy on the gates assumed they were leaving for a genuine mission like always," said Graham.

"Shit!" shouted Dave.

Dave was still mostly dressed in his clothes from the

night before as it was rarely warm enough to go to bed without them. He leapt to his feet, slipped his boots on and ran downstairs. The ground floor of the house was empty when breakfast would usually be happening, something no man or woman would miss. He could already hear a ruckus outside. He ran out of the front door to see Roger and several others arguing.

"What the hell's going on here?" asked Dave.

"Tommy, Richard, Brian and Chris have taken your truck, and these idiots let them do it," said Roger.

"How were we supposed to know they weren't allowed out?" asked Amy.

"Alright, alright. That doesn't matter, how long ago did this happen?" asked Dave.

"About forty minutes ago," said Jodie.

"Shit, he could be anywhere by now!" said Dave.

"Really? Surely you know what his intentions were?" asked Roger.

Dave thought about it. It was indeed true that he had an idea, the conversation from the night before flooded back into his head. The possibility that Tommy had been stupid enough to go ahead with the idea was depressing, and to risk so many of the survivors foolhardy and selfish.

"There's a supermarket about fifty miles from here, he's been raving about wanting to raid it for a while," said Dave.

"Exactly," said Roger.

"Shit," said Luke.

Roger's other right hand man had arrived on the scene just seconds after Dave. Luke was a competent and reliable fellow, but also a gun hoe one.

"Let's get after them and drag their arses back!" shouted Luke.

"No, we have no idea what they've got themselves into, we have already lost four men and two vehicles today, let's not risk any others!" said Roger.

"What if they need our help?" asked Jodie.

"Then they're probably in too much trouble for us to assist them, either they come back here okay or not at all, it's out of our hands now," said Roger.

"This is bollocks," said Dave.

"Yes it is, Dave. But there's nothing more we can do about it without knowing more. None of us know how many survivors there are in this world, but all of us are very aware that it's a very small number. The very survival of the human race is in danger, and we cannot afford to take stupid risks," said Roger.

He was right, none of them wanted to condemn these friends to their deaths but Roger had, as always, proven why he was the right man to control the group. Roger didn't have much in the way of skills, but he was always cool headed no matter the situation, his calculated thinking and nerve had got them all this far.

"Right, those not on watch get some breakfast, we will

pray for the four men but beyond that, life goes on," said Roger.

The group broke apart and went about their morning routine. The loss of the men and vehicles was weighing heavily on all of their minds. The number of survivors was ever decreasing. The only way for that to turn around would be for people to stop being foolish, and of course for some to start having children. There was no doubt that Roger's leadership and facilities had provided a safe life for all, but they had to keep improving.

After finishing his breakfast, Dave went on watch with the guard at the gate, out of desperation rather than duty. The guard tower at the entrance was an old tractor with a guard station built on the roof. The rusty Massey Ferguson tractor had belonged to Roger's father, but was long beyond operation now. Dave sat in the tower with Jodie and Kyle for an hour without speaking a word to either of them. There was a deathly silence across the whole camp now, all too depressed by the loss of their friends, a reminder of how brutal the outside world still was.

Finally, after the long wait the group could hear the sound of an engine in the distance, the sound of a Land Rover engine. The vehicle was clearly being driven hard. Eventually it came into view but the second vehicle wasn't with it. Jodie jumped to use the church bell that had been setup there to alert the camp of anything serious.

"No!" shouted Dave.

Jodie looked quickly at Dave in shock. She couldn't understand his reasoning. The sight of the vehicle had been a joyous sight, all sensibilities melted away.

"That bell alerts everything in the valley, not just our camp, that is for emergencies only," said Dave.

He jumped down from the tower.

"Roger, Kate is back!" shouted Dave.

Roger didn't look particularly enthusiastic. The fact that one vehicle had returned rather than two was a bad sign. Despite the fact that the vehicle had returned, he knew all too well that this could lead to a number of unfortunate and dangerous situations. Dave wrenched the gates open and his beloved Land Rover pulled into the camp. Brian was driving but there was no sign of any passengers.

He stopped the vehicle and leapt out. Before his feet could barely touch the ground, Luke had pounced on him. The hardy captain threw him against the side of the vehicle in anger.

"What the hell did you think you were doing?" shouted Luke.

"Luke! Let him speak!" shouted Dave.

Luke released his hold on the man. Roger stood back and simply waited for the bad news, praying that further survivors would not be pulled into this disaster.

"Where are the others?" asked Dave.

"We went to the supermarket in the town and it was all

fine and quiet. But once the lads got inside the place was just flooded with zombies, there was nothing I could do!" shouted Brian.

"So you just left them there?" asked Dave.

"I was outside in the truck, there were dozens of them, more all the time, what was I supposed to do?" asked Brian.

"You were supposed to do as you were told in the first place!" shouted Luke.

"Fuck you! We were trying to make things better for all of us!" shouted Brian.

"And now you can understand the very reason we do things my way," said Roger.

"So where are the guys now?" asked Dave.

"They said on the radio they were held up in the security room and it was fairly safe for now, but the shop is flooded with creatures," said Brian.

"Then there's nothing we can do for them, they condemned themselves," said Roger.

"Fuck that, we can't afford to lose anyone, we're too few already!" shouted Dave.

"And we'll be even fewer if you attempt some ridiculous rescue attempt!" shouted Roger.

"I don't need your permission," said Dave.

"Please, Dave. You should know as well as I how futile this is," said Roger.

"Surely our concern for our fellow man, our hope and

comradeship is what makes us human? We don't have much else left," said Dave.

Roger thought for a minute about the situation. He knew that it was very dangerous to risk any resources on a rescue attempt, but he also knew that the morale of his people was on a knife edge now.

"Then what did you have in mind?" asked Roger.

"Let me take Kate and Brian. If we don't return, don't come after us, but if we do, be ready with the whiskey," said Dave.

"You think you can do this with two men and one vehicle?" asked Luke.

"I think I can do it in such a way that more men would provide no extra safety," said Dave.

"Okay, I don't like it, but if risking just a little more can return this community to what it was, so be it, you have my blessing," said Roger.

"Okay, Brian, how much fuel we got in Kate?" asked Dave.

"Half a tank," said Brian.

"Great, then do whatever you have to do be ready, I'll be back here in two minutes. We'll set off immediately," said Dave.

He ran back into the house and up to his equipment in the room he'd slept in the night before. Just a minute later he was geared up and ready to go. He grabbed his club hammer, his close range weapon of choice. In reality he would prefer a larger two hand weapon, but the fact he spent much of his time in vehicles and other confined spaces meant they weren't always practical. He ran back downstairs and to the hallway of the house, heading for the door, when he was stopped by Kailey blocking his way. She looked tearful and scared.

"You don't have to do this you know," said Kailey.

"Yes, I do, I'm sorry, but we'll make it back," said Dave.

"Nothing I can do will make you stay?" asked Kailey.

"No, just keep the home fires burning and don't let spirits drop any further," said Dave.

Kailey reached forward and kissed him, before moving aside to let him pass. It was the huge boost in confidence that Dave needed to go into a zombie infested situation. Never before had he deliberately headed towards a horde of zombies. There would be no logical reason to do so under normal circumstances. Dave and Brian mounted up in the Land Rover and spun it around to again leave the compound.

"Good luck," said Roger.

"Thanks, we'll do what we can," said Dave.

"Don't get cocky, you know even the best of us can only handle a few of these animals at once, they'll wear you down and swamp you," said Luke.

"Thanks. If we aren't back in three hours, assume we failed," said Dave.

The gates were pulled back and Dave drove the vehicle

out of the compound. Normally he sat in the passenger seat acting as commander and navigator, but this time he wanted full control of the vehicle.

"So what's the plan?" asked Brian.

"Firstly, from now on you follow my orders, not Tommy's, or either of the other silly fuckers who went on this stupid arse mission," said Dave.

"Alright, I'm sorry," said Brian.

"Sorry? I don't want you to be sorry, I want you to stop fucking up, risking the lives of our friends, which you did in not listening to those of us that know better!" shouted Dave.

"Okay, got ya," said Brian.

The man looked sheepish, but then he should have. He was lucky that his fellow survivors hadn't beaten him for being so foolish. They only didn't because each valued the physical condition of one another too much. Brian now shut up, the best thing he could do.

"For a start we have no chance of fighting however many there are there, and I don't know a way of safely drawing them away," said Dave.

"So what do we do?" asked Brian.

"How well do you know the shop layout?" asked Dave.

"Very well, I used to go there every weekend before all this shit started," said Brian.

"Good, then we're going to ram the fuckers," said Dave.

"Sounds good," said Brian.

"We have enough metal and torque to break through the numbers that are likely to be in our way. You need to tell me exactly how we can smash through the outer walls and where the office is," said Dave.

"The only way in is through the front door, it's the only place without crash barriers up, once you're in the office is a straight route to the back of the building," said Brian.

"Alright, then we use speed and power, nothing else. You'll be in the back of the truck ready to open the door, we do not waste a single second," said Dave.

"Alright," said Brian.

"Also, when we get within a mile of the shop, you radio them and explain the plan," said Dave.

An hour later they were just a few minutes away from the supermarket. It had been an anxious journey so far, both men concerned not just for the three they were trying to rescue, but also their own lives. The entire mission was a gamble. No sensible person would ever go near such a crowd of beasts. Brian lifted up the radio handset.

"Tommy, come in. This is Brian, I repeat, this is Brian. Can anyone hear me?" he asked.

"This is Tommy, what the fuck is going on?" he asked.

"The horde struck and I had to leave, but we have a plan. We're driving straight to you, be ready to move!" said Brian.

"What's your ETA?" asked Tommy.

"One minute, be ready," said Brian.

"Right, now get in the back and hold onto something. Make sure you have a weapon close to hand, as it's going to be a mad rush getting those three in," said Dave.

A minute later they were entering the car park of the supermarket. They drove all the way to the entrance, a handful of zombies were in the area stumbling towards the building. The shutters of the building were up and the glass electric doors prized open. The Land Rover passed through the first entrance and then smashed through the second, simply too large to fit the door frame.

Dave could already see the mass of creatures packed in tight along the aisle that led to the office. He had carefully manoeuvred the vehicle into the building, but there was no more time or need for careful and restrained driving. Dave put his foot to the floor, knowing that torque alone may not be enough to keep moving through such a mass.

The two tonne vehicle ploughed into the rear of the zombie crowd, bodies buckling against the thick bull bar. Zombies were thrown off onto the shelves to the side of the truck. Dave kept his foot to the floor as the shelves beside them were being pushed outwards, unable to contain the expanding horde as the Land Rover forced itself through them. He could finally see the office door up ahead. The number of creatures was far too many to simply stop and let their friends in. He swung the vehicle off down the end of the aisle and slammed the brakes on, sliding to a halt as they crushed further more zombies.

The gearbox squealed as Dave slammed it into reverse before they had even come quite to a stop. He put his foot back down hard on the accelerator and smashed the vehicle backwards into the security office. The door flew off its hinges and the truck smashed half the wall down with it. Brian swung the door open whilst the zombies were already swarming around the vehicle. He jumped out.

"Get the fuck in!" shouted Brian.

The three men, still in shock from the audacious rescue attempt stumbled towards the vehicle. Brian noticed the first creature was already within a dangerous distance. He picked up his hatchet and drove it into the target's head. The three men clambered into the back.

"Go!" shouted Brian.

Dave immediately put the power down, already concerned that the mass of creatures could stop them from getting moving again. Fortunately, many of the beasts had approached from the direction they'd come and were now mostly flooding the side of the vehicle, rather than the front. Brian jumped in as the wheels had already begun moving.

The truck smashed through the zombies before it, breaking bones and sending blood splattering across the bonnet and windscreen. They stormed down the next aisle which was mostly clear. Brian looked distraught to see so much in the way of food supplies being passed by. This place was exactly the cheese in the trap situation which Roger had always warned them about. They all now wished that each and every member of the group had heeded his words.

They reached the end of the aisle and Dave swung the wheel around, sliding the vehicle round the tight bend. The rear quarter of the truck smashed into an aisle of tin cans. The impact was barely noticeable in the vehicle, its sheer weight passing through the mass of small objects. A few seconds later they had reached the entrance of the building. They crashed into the tail end of the horde, and over the crumpled bodies they'd left on entering.

Finally natural light hit the windscreen as they broke out into the car park. Reaching daylight and open air was always a relief in this zombie infested land. Dave slowed the vehicle to a more cruising speed and set about getting home. For ten minutes they all sat silently, the rescuers happy to have survived, the rescued men feeling too guilty to say a word. Finally, Tommy leant forward into the front cab of the truck.

"Thank you, Dave," he said.

"Just don't underestimate what a fuck up this was, it was sheer luck that everyone got out of there alive," said Dave.

"I'm sorry," said Tommy.

"You bloody well should be, but save it for Roger, he'll give you the grilling you deserve. I'm sure," said Dave.

The survivors again went quiet and remained so for the rest of the journey. It was a solemn drive, each one of them reflecting on the near disastrous day that could have been. Dave was only heartened by the fact that these events may have taught the men a valuable lesson, and without any cost in lives.

They finally reached the entrance to Everglade, it was in part a triumphant return, but also depressing. Their victory had achieved nothing. They had no further supplies, nothing of any worth. The gates were pulled back and the group in the Land Rover could already see that the entire population of the facility was waiting for them, a rare sight. Their fellow survivors were cheering, seeing that more had returned than had left two hours earlier. Only one man among them all looked unhappy, Roger. He stood, arms crossed, fuming.

Dave drew the vehicle to a halt and got out as Brian opened up the door to let out their passengers. They were welcomed with much applause and back patting. The entire group was happy, smiling and laughing, an ecstasy that was unknown to these people since the Zompoc began.

"Silence!" shouted Roger.

The ecstatic shouts of the crowd calmed and all turned their attention to Roger. It was a difficult thing for the survivors to comprehend, that during this time of sheer joy and relief that they would have to face the seriousness of Roger's strict command.

"Dave did a wonderful thing, something I myself never thought possible and he should be praised for it. But none of you should underestimate the sheer idiotic actions which led to these events. The fact that Dave has brought these men back to us would largely be based on luck, and despite all of his heroic deeds, they have returned with nothing new."

The crowd was subdued by the reality check that Roger had brought upon them. In the horrific year that the men and women of Everglade had survived, any sign or evidence of hope and success was welcome, but Roger was now dashing their hopes. Roger knew that morale was important, but he also knew that an unrealistic idea of life was now a dangerous characteristic to hold.

"Let this be a lesson to you all. It's easy to pursue the obvious pleasures that may be in front of you, and don't any of you think I haven't thought the same. Everything I have ever done for this group has been with the right intentions, for us all to survive in the best way we can. Many things we do in life now are a risk, but I calculate risk carefully, and since you have been here, not a single person has died, is that not proof enough of my capability in leadership?" asked Roger.

The group of survivors murmured and hummed amongst themselves, none willing to commit to a response with their eccentric leader. All of them knew that the middle aged and odd fellow was right, he planned too well not to be, but none wanted to either question or agree with him.

"All of you. Take stock in the fact that you are all still alive, safe, fed and warm. By these modern standards, we all live a life of luxury, and you remember that next time any one of you has a crazy idea like Tommy's," said Roger.

It was enough for the crowd to understand, Roger full well knew the limitations of the group. Few individuals understood what was necessary for them all to live safely, but that was what made his role so vital among these men and women.

"That's enough now but remember today, it's an important lesson, now go about your tasks, ever remembering the risks that face us," said Roger.

The group sighed, suddenly saddened by the grim reality shock that their leader had given them. They dispersed and went about their daily business. The day went on in its usual fashion. Life on a day-to-day basis required effort in order to stay physically and mentally stimulated. Those who went out of Everglade to forage for supplies had a specific job to do in life, an adventure of a sort. For the rest of the populace, life revolved around keeping watch over the facility, preparing food, and keeping the community clean and healthy.

The night passed on without incident, just as the community had become accustomed. The following day, Dave arose to again go out into the zombie world to procure the supplies necessary for keep them all alive. What he would give for a Burger King meal could simply not be explained. Roger did what he could to keep life interesting in Everglade. Sadly, there was no substitute for going out into a bustling town for an evening of entertainment. The lack of electricity meant that they could have no TV, the fuel was considered too valuable, keeping the generators for emergency usage only.

CHAPTER FIVE

MID-WEST, UNITED STATES

It was a mild evening and Madison sat rocking in her chair. She could just about hear the sounds of her father's sermon echoing around the walls of their church. He would blindly live under the assumption that his daughter was always on the important duties of defending their community, that she had duties which kept her from his services. In reality, she sat cradling her AK47, looking out across the open plains.

It had taken months of bloodshed to purge their small town of the zombie menace, that her father Richard Wells called the Devil's minions. Ever since that time she enjoyed what quiet and peaceful time she could get.

The small town's old name was cast aside with the rebirth of the place, like the phoenix her father had told her. The shelter they now lived in they called Babylon. Of the thousands who had lived there, only fifty five now inhabited the area. No walls had ever been built around their homes, only the individual defences of each building, as they were all too far apart to easily create boundary walls.

Babylon was miles from anywhere that had previously contained people, a natural defence which the community relied upon, supported by regular patrols and thick bars on their windows and doors. Wells would never have them build walls, he said the living should never have to live within the prison confines of their own town and that they would use their labour to maintain a free society. For this reason no alcohol was allowed, and every man and woman was to be armed and ready at all times.

The silence was broken as Madison heard the sound of someone climbing her watch tower, the clumsy noise of a man stumbling as his slung rifle bashed against the ladder. This was the familiar sound of Justin. He appeared at the top.

"Hey Maddy, what's happening?" he asked.

She acted politely, but was more than a little annoyed that her peaceful evening had been interrupted. Justin was a capable fighter but simple minded, and only ever interested in how many women he could bed, which was growing ever more difficult in the small and close knit community.

"Hey, Justin, why aren't you at service?" asked Madison.

"Oh come on, it bores me to death, what's your excuse?" asked Justin.

"I'm on watch," said Madison.

"Convenient that whenever services are held you're up here," said Justin.

"He's my father, I already know what he's going to tell you all, I hear it the rest of the day!" said Madison.

The glint of some movement in the distance caught her eye. She stood up and squinted to make it out. Her sight confirmed what her heart already knew, a zombie staggered down the main road towards their homes. A crossroads at the church meant that they could be approached from four sides, but fences and walls in all homes and side roads meant that everything was channelled down the main long roads. This meant the management of defences and survivors was simple, without having to live within walls.

"We've got one," said Madison.

"Shit, that's the first one in a week!" shouted Justin.

He leapt to his feet to look out down the open road. Unslinging his rifle from his shoulder, Justin peered down the hunting scope at the creature.

"Looks like a city boy!" he said.

"Yeah, I look forward to the day when the creatures stop coming to find us," said Madison.

"Yeah, how do you think they do that?" asked Justin.

"I dunno, there's so many out there maybe it's just

luck, or maybe they can smell us from thousands of miles away," said Madison.

"I'd love to shoot this bitch right here and now, one shot through the fucking eye," said Justin.

"No, no, not with a gun!" shouted Madison.

"I know, just saying," said Justin.

Madison propped her AK47 against the wall of the tower and picked up the crossbow next to it. The entire community owned guns, at least one, whether they had them before the Zompoc began, or found them afterwards. However, Babylon had a simple policy, guns were for emergency use only and the weapons with easily replenishable supplies should always be used. A simple routine cull of a single creature or two like this would never necessitate the use of a gun. A silent weapon was also favourable, as it didn't break the peace and quiet that the town and parish so eagerly protected.

The zombie was a hundred yards away when Madison slammed the crossbow stirrup down onto the floor and put her foot through it. She pulled the string back until it locked into place on the trigger. Standing up, she slipped the bolt onto the track and laid the rifle crossbow to rest on the wall. She pulled her chair closer and sat down on it, providing the most comfortable and steady position she could for shooting.

Peering down the scope at her target, Madison could see the creature used to be an office worker, the typical simple grey suit, now ripped and ragged. The shirt was so stained with dry blood, dust and grime that it was hard to tell it used to be white. She took careful aim at the beast's skull through the red dot sight and then finely squeezed the trigger, whilst Justin still watched through his rifle scope.

The bolt skewed the zombie through the eye socket, a well placed shot. The two watched as the creature staggered on a few extra steps whilst spasming, until it collapsed to the ground, finally lifeless, this time for good.

"Fucking right on!" shouted Justin.

Madison looked over at him with a grin. Despite his annoying her, she was satisfied by the applause of the crowd she had, revelling in her martial skill. She noticed lights appear in the distance, the artificial light at night that only manmade technology could make. She picked up the binoculars hanging from her chair and looked out down the long flat road.

"It's the hunters!" shouted Madison.

The town organised regular missions to gather supplies from afar, essential items such as ammunition, medical supplies and food products which they could not grow themselves. These parties were called 'hunters', as they were in the traditional sense, hunter gatherers. The hunters were the only people allowed to use cars, except in cases of emergency. Madison took hold of the bell ringer hanging off the side of the tower and gave two bells, the signal that friendlies were approaching.

The doors of the church swung open, the light from the candles beaming out into the street was quickly followed by the congregation, led by Wells. The three pickup trucks pulled up outside the church, each one armoured across its cab and with supplies in their beds. The door opened on the first vehicle and out stepped Jack, he was the leader of the hunter teams. Jack had no farming skills at all, but had served in the Marine Corps straight from school, making him naturally suited to the job.

Richard Wells trotted forward with his usual enthusiasm, always treating the hunters like their saviours after returning from any mission, an important task to maintain morale he said. He stepped forward and offered out his hand to Jack, patting him on the back. Jack took the gesture of good will, but didn't look particularly happy.

"Well done boys, another fine job! And I see God did not let any harm come to you!" shouted Wells.

"No, but we didn't come back with a whole load either," said Jack.

"I can see you have brought back a worthy haul, and that's all that can be asked of you," said Wells.

"It doesn't change the fact that these supplies are becoming more and more difficult to find, with us having to travel further all the time," said Jack.

"Let's not worry about the troubles of tomorrow, when we have success and much to celebrate today. Let's get these trucks unloaded and sit down for supper!" shouted Wells.

The crowd cheered, appeased by the welcoming notion of a warm meal in their bellies. Wells continually kept spirits high by preaching the bible on a daily basis and re-enforcing it with food and entertainment for the group. Plays and stage performances were common, providing they contained good Christian values. Card games were allowed to pass the time, but not with any form of gambling involved. It was a pure and simple life that the group led, and whilst it was at many times boring and drab, they were all thankful to still be living. The men began unloading supplies whilst Wells retired to his home for a short rest before supper.

"Madison, please join me," he said.

She followed her father back to their home, which they had shared since the outbreak began. Her father was tired, exhausted by the daily work and routine of having to manage, motivate and entertain their community. He sat down with a huff at their dining table.

"Would you like a coffee, father?" asked Madison.

Her AK47 was still slung from her shoulder. Wells looked up at her with his tired eyes, shaking his head at the sight of her weapon.

"You know that there are better roles you can serve here than that," said Wells.

"But every person here must carry a weapon at all

times," said Madison.

"No, not that, you spend all of your time with rifle in hand, in watch towers, patrolling the perimeter," said Wells.

"That's what we need," she said.

"There are plenty of men who would be quite up to the task. We're a small community as it is, do you not think it's time you married one of the fine young men and brought new life into this world?" asked Wells.

She slammed the coffee mug down on the worktop where she was preparing the drink for her father. It was indeed true that she was among the minority of the group, being a young, fit and healthy female, but the suggestion did not at all meet with her idea of life.

"I don't want to marry and I don't want children. Is it not enough, the work I do for this town?" she asked.

"No, sadly it is not. In this world we must forget what we want and do our duty. We all have to make sacrifices. You are one of only a handful in Babylon who can spawn the next generation, or we will all grow old and weak with no one to defend us and carry on the Lord's work," said Wells.

"And what is the Lord's work?" shouted Madison.

"My dear daughter, I thought you understood by now. It is life, to live life according to good moral and principle practice, which is largely to pro-create and keep evil at arm's length. You are doing a fine work of the latter, but it is time you let others take on that responsibility and do what few can. You will again do the work you do now, once your children are teenagers themselves," said Wells.

Madison walked across the room and ripped the door open, furious at her father's insights. She knew in her heart that he was right, but it seemed so unfair, beyond levels she could yet accept.

"I am not having children!" shouted Madison.

She slammed the door and strutted down the street towards the dining hall. She already knew that she would have to accept her father's wishes, not only because he was her father and Babylon's leader, but because their survival as a community depended on it in the long term. But she would hold on to her current life as long as she possibly could. Since the Zompoc began she had finally had a true purpose and role, beyond the toil of everyday life in the safe old world, and she wouldn't let anyone take that from her.

Madison reached the restaurant that had become the community's dining hall, big enough for all of the survivors to sit in at any one time, though they never would. Eight people remained on watch at all times, two at each road leading to the intersection. She stepped through the door to be hit with the warm heat and light of the oil lamp lit room and the sound of joyous discussion. Most of the community was already assembled, whilst the smell of their supper cooking wafting around the room. The meals they ate generally consisted of a combination of stews and soups, because they were easy to make in large quantity with whichever ingredients were available at the time. Madison walked over to a table near Jack, who she held in high regard having been childhood friends, and pulled up a chair to his table. He would like nothing more than to marry and settle down with Madison, but was always too busy and aware of the impending work and caution needed to give it consideration or pursuit. Jack was sitting with three of his friends, all of a similar age, the men that hunted with him.

"Hey Jack, how's life?" asked Madison.

"So, so," he said.

"How come?" asked Madison.

"We didn't come back with half as much as I would have liked, my truck is misfiring and I could kill for a beer," said Jack.

"It could be worse," said Madison.

"Really, you're sure about that? Afghanistan sucked, but at least we always knew we had home to go back to. This sucks as bad, with no hope of a better future."

"Oh come on, you can't talk like that, we're doing great. We're alive and we have each other," said Madison.

"Mmm, it's better than being a zombie, I'll grant you that," said Jack.

The night went on in much the same fashion as it had started. Most of the people in the community lived blindly in a happy but simple life, whilst Pastor Wells exhausted himself physically and mentally to achieve and maintain their high spirits. Meantime, those having to venture out into the rest of the world were being beaten down by the depressing and tragic sights they had to see each and every day, of ghost towns and decaying bodies, whether they were still walking or not.

Those with the true insight into the world's situation were all too aware that life was only getting more difficult, with what was manufactured in the old world getting ever rarer, and the number of enemies staying constant.

Halfway through the evening Pastor Wells stepped out from the room and into the kitchen. He returned a few moments later holding several bottles of wine.

"Ladies and Gentleman!" shouted Wells.

The crowd went silent and turned their attention to Wells, all surprised to see an alcoholic beverage anywhere in sight.

"I have always been insistent that we remain alcohol free in Babylon, not because the Lord wills it or the bible tells us so, neither have any issue with alcohol in moderation. Our rules have been in place so that we can all remain alive! However, we have now survived a year in this new world, a world occupied by evil. We have beaten all the odds, stuck together, and achieved a sturdy and lively community. Let us all share a glass of wine together in celebration, as you have all earned it!" said Wells.

The crowd erupted with laughter, quickly taking the bottles and passing them around. Each man and woman filled their cups as high as they could go until the bottles were empty. Finally, they sat quietly, impatiently and with all attention on the Pastor, waiting for his approval.

"Now, let us drink to our fallen friends, our living comrades, to the grace of God and the abolition of evil!" shouted Wells.

The people all stood and raised their glasses before taking their first sips. Jack sat down with a sigh, he was clearly unimpressed by the gesture, though his dissatisfaction went unnoticed by the Pastor, but not to Madison.

"What's wrong, it's what you wanted isn't it?" asked Madison.

"No, I said a beer, but that's not the point. Your father would never give out alcohol in this day and age unless he considered it vital to morale, meaning, there are cracks appearing in the community," said Jack.

"Maybe he just thought we could all do with a relaxing evening and a reward for our work?" asked Madison.

"No, it's not the way the Pastor works. He's methodical, he makes actions for the greater good, not conscience or instinct," said Jack.

"Yeah, tell me about it," said Madison.

"What is it?" asked Jack.

"Nothing, just him being his usual self," said Madison.

"Well, let's at least enjoy this drink while we have it,"

said Jack.

It was a solemn evening for those who knew more about the life and workings of Babylon than the majority, knowing that this was the best it would get, and that it wouldn't be repeated often. Wells again rose to speak, his audience were already silent before he had fully stood up.

"We've had a long and hard year, I will not deny it, but you have all done well and continue to do so. On Saturday we will have a baseball game, for all to watch. In fact, we'll have two, and cycle the sentries so that everyone has a turn to either play or watch," he said.

The crowd again cheered at their leader's speech, clawing at any hope or fun that they could possibly find in their lives. The evening came to a close and Madison went back to her watch tower to join the guard who was in it. It was not her turn for duty, but she couldn't tolerate returning home to her father that night.

CHAPTER SIX

ENGLAND

Nick pushed the gearstick into fourth as the Land Rover picked up speed on the wide six-lane carriageway. He was only doing twenty miles per hour but with the amount of debris scattered across the lanes, any faster would have been suicidal. It was amazing that after just a few months the road had deteriorated so badly with holes, debris, abandoned vehicles and possessions.

Nick led the convoy of eight vehicles in a long, scattered column across the deserted debris ridden motorway though the heart of England. He drove a late nineties model Defender, the same kind of vehicle used by British forces in Afghanistan just a few years ago. It was of a similar size to an American Chevy Silverado. It was a tough, utilitarian four-wheel drive and hadn't seen any serious changes in design since the sixties. The Defender had been modified in several ways to make it useful and reliable in these exceptional circumstances. The first addition was the wheel protection made up of hanging metal slats over the tyres to stop damage from wrecked cars and possible raiders. The doors and windows were covered in thick mesh and sliding metal shutters. The front of the vehicle was taken up with a large steel snow plough and the roof contained an improved weapon platform with a hatch that led down to the front passenger seat. It was heavy, tough and easily maintained, perfect for use in an apocalypse.

Looking out of the small rectangular windscreen Nick could see cars and trucks littering the sides of the road. At some point a large number of them had been pushed out of the way, but even now some still forced him to slow down. With a clump the hatch above him on the roof lifted open and Artur, a young Polish man lowered his head inside.

"We've got something in the road up ahead," he called.

Nick nodded as he pulled the handset from the radio that was tied with plastic cable ties to the damaged and worn dashboard. He keyed the radio, holding the microphone up to his face.

"Hammer One, this is Hammer Three, we've got something up ahead," said Nick.

There was a short pause, punctuated by static. As he waited for a response he checked the map attached to the dashboard. They'd left the outskirts of London in the early hours of the morning, having collected survivors and supplies from the Hammersmith Rescue Centre. The trip should technically only take two hours back to the Green Zone but since the Zompoc the trip now took up most of the day. Even worse was that if they hit a problem then they would be forced to take cover for the night. Being caught out of the Green Zone after dark was a big problem and one the convoy avoided at all costs.

"Hammer Three, we're slowing the convoy, check it out. Hammer Two will join you," came the response.

"Roger," answered Nick as he replaced the mic back on the dashboard.

Nick checked his side mirrors, noting the half a dozen vehicles behind him were slowing down. Only one, a small bus that was heavily modified stayed with him. At first glance it looked like a conventional bus, but closer examination revealed the windows were boarded up with reinforced metal shutters and it had masses of supplies and boxes on its roof. There were weapon mounts fitted at the front and back of the vehicle with hatches leading back inside. A man was sitting at the front weapon mount, turning the firearm as he scanned the surrounding area.

Looking ahead down the long stretch of motorway, Nick steered the Land Rover through debris. He was extra careful to avoid anything that could damage the tyres or underside of the vehicle. They had learned the hard way that all vehicles hit trouble once they sustained damage to their wheels. Unlike in the movies, a simple glass bottle could shred a tyre and leave you stranded and vulnerable.

The two vehicles weaved past several heaps of debris and then slowed as they approached an area with scores of crashed and burnt cars. These were different to other wrecked cars they'd seen on the motorway. A few were still smoking and some of them looked like they'd been carrying supplies. After a clear section on the motorway there was a thick plume of black smoke ahead.

"Approaching a Z-Zone," said Nick on the handset.

Nick turned to Artur.

"Get ready, I don't like it, this could be trouble," he ordered.

Artur looked confused. He'd only been on a few runs with the convoy and this was the first time he'd come across this term.

"Z-Zone?" he asked, as he checked his weapons.

"Yeah, you don't see so many of them now. Back at the start you'd get a whole section of road blocked off by a few crashed cars. Once the road was blocked the rest of the traffic would get stuck and people would abandon their cars. The zombies would come and start attacking them and have easy pickings in the panic," explained Nick.

Artur opened up several cases in the back of the Land Rover as he pulled out more ammunition for their weapons, anticipating possible trouble ahead.

"What happened after the zombies attacked?" he asked.

"In a few hours the road would be deserted apart from the vehicles, supplies and bodies. You used to be able to spot them by the car fires that would spread to anything nearby that was flammable. There were times when we found hundreds of cars and probably up to a thousand dead outside some cities," answered Nick.

Artur lifted himself back up so that he could see out of the hatch that had been cut into the roof of the Land Rover. It was roughly done and the edges were covered in a piece of green garden hose so he wouldn't be cut as he moved about. On top of the vehicle, attached to a metal mounting was a vintage World War II Bren gun. This distinctive light machine gun was a staple weapon of the British Empire and this particular one had been deactivated for a long time. The workers back at the compound had reworked it heavily and added new parts so that it was once again functional. The modification of weapons and supply of ammunition was a real issue, but the vehicles of the convoys always got priority. One very handy modification was the fitting of a large spotting scope on a mount next to the main gun. It meant Artur could spot possible targets from a long distance away. Artur pulled back the bolt and then swung the weapon around as he scanned the surroundings. From his position he could see a coach about three hundred metres ahead. He banged his hand on the roof of the Land Rover, Nick shouted back up.

"Yeah, I see it. Get ready," he ordered.

Sound came through the radio's speakers from one of the vehicles.

"Any update on the route? Is it a Z-Zone?" crackled the voice.

The Land Rover slowed down to almost a walking pace as the two vehicles moved cautiously towards the smoke plume. As they reached the two hundred metre distance they could make out a crashed coach and at least three other large vehicles. They were all badly damaged and all looked heavily modified, much like their own vehicles. More importantly, they were completely blocking the road ahead for the convoy.

"We have multiple vehicles blocking the route. Looks like another convoy came this way," said Nick.

With a squeal the Land Rover came to a stop. Nick leaned forward slightly and pulled out a double-barrelled hammer-lock shotgun. The weapon had been shortened at some point, but even this modification failed to make the vintage weapon look even close to a modern firearm. Nick pulled the lever and broke the weapon's barrel to expose the chambers. Placing his hand in his combat vest he pulled out two red cartridges and slipped them into the gun. With a click the weapon was ready and he took the portable radio off its mount and slipped it onto his belt. He then slid back the steel shutter and opened the door, the smoke from the fires quickly entering his nostrils.

Artur heard the door opening and swung his Bren gun around to cover the abandoned vehicles. The weapon swung quickly around on its heavy, metal mounting.

Nick stepped out, holding the shotgun up to his shoulder and looked around at the scene of carnage. He could count five vehicles. Each one was heavily modified with extra cargo straps, racks, reinforced windows and mounts for weapons. The armoured bus stopped close to the Land Rover, the two vehicles forming a 'v' shape in the road. The air operated doors swung open to reveal the dark interior of the bus. Four men stepped out, each heavily armed with firearms, crossbows and close-quarters weapons. They moved forwards, meeting up with Nick.

Standing out at the front, a noise caught his attention from the embankment on the side of the road. The first thought that entered his mind was that this could be an ambush. He dropped to one knee and aimed the shotgun in the direction of the sound. A few more sounds came from the same direction, but before he could move one of the vehicles in the middle of the road started to shake. He gave a hand signal and without a word the men around him fanned out. The two on the left moved to the embankment whilst the other two approached the crashed vehicles.

From the top of the Land Rover, Artur had a perfect view of the scene. He could see the two groups examining the area whilst Nick watched. He heard another sound coming from inside the bus and he swung the Bren around just in time to spot three scrawny looking people stumble out of the damaged rear door. At first glance it looked like the people were starving survivors, but Artur knew better. A closer look revealed the torn clothing and blood drooling faces that were the distinctive marks of the undead. Even after a year these creatures were still moving and their bodies were not decaying as they had first suspected they would. Of course there was a good chance that these were newly made zombies, if so then they had to be very careful. Artur had found out the hard way what happened when people you knew were made into zombies.

Without hesitating he aimed carefully and squeezed the trigger. Nothing happened.

"Shit," muttered Artur, as he pulled out the magazine and checked for the jam. He looked up, spotting the creatures shambling out into the road and directly towards Nick.

"Incoming!" shouted Artur pointing to the group moving into the road.

Nick heard Artur and quickly turned, swinging around to his right until he was facing the bus. Three of the creatures were heading towards him, each of them was badly injured, either from previous fighting or possibly from the crash on the motorway. Without hesitation he pulled the first trigger of the shotgun and emptied a custom shell into the group. These shells were all handmade as was all the ammunition for the convoy guards. They were designed to cause maximum trauma to flesh whilst having almost no ability to penetrate armour or very thick clothing. Whilst this reduced their ability against living targets they were perfect for shooting the undead.

The closest of the zombies took the first blast directly in the chest. The specially design lead shot tore through the creature's chest and burst out of its back. The metal shot ripped the decayed organs apart and severed the spinal column, collapsing the creature to a lifeless lump of flesh. A few of the stray pieces of shot struck the other two but caused no harm. The man to his right fired several shots with his revolver, two of them hitting one of the zombies in the leg, it dropped down but continued to drag itself forward.

As Nick pulled the second trigger on the shotgun the two remaining zombies flew backwards into the bus, inch sized holes appearing in their torsos and multiple holes appeared in the vehicle behind them. The heavy thud of the Bren followed almost immediately. Each of the large calibre bullets tore chunks out of the creatures and both were splattered against the metal work.

Nick turned back and gave a thumbs up signal to Artur. He then pulled out the radio and lifted it to his mouth.

"Hammer One, there's Z activity in the area," said Nick.

As before there was a short delay whilst the radio crackled. The rest of the convoy was only a kilometre behind them but they were finding with no line of sight the signal dropped off very fast.

"Shit. Are you okay? Any casualties?" came the crackling reply.

Nick looked around, making sure nothing else was close to him.

"Negative, there was only a handful, we're still scouting the area," he said.

"Be careful, clear the road if feasible, if not we'll take the backup route," said the man on the radio.

"Shit," whispered Nick to himself. He was not happy at the prospect of having to take a detour. This meant using a less substantial road that could easily be blocked or damaged in some way.

Artur shouted something but Nick couldn't hear due to the next message on the radio.

"Roger, keep us appraised of the situation, we're sending a scout unit back to check on the last exit in case we need to find a new route.

"Understood," answered Nick as he placed the radio onto his belt.

He turned back to Artur.

"Yeah?" he asked.

"I can see more zombies behind the bus," said Artur in a matter-of-fact tone.

Nick pulled out another two shells and slipped them into the now empty chambers. As he broke open the barrel a waft of smoke drifted out. He was always wary of using the gun. It made noise and noise usually attracted attention, something that was never a good thing.

"How many?" he asked.

"Not many, about two dozen, I think," answered Artur.

The two men to his right were waiting, ready for his signal. He looked over to his left, the other two men were halfway up the embankment and watching down for signs of trouble. With another hand signal he directed them to move forwards and past the vehicles. They each crept forward, both trying to get past the wrecked vehicles quickly but also careful of what could be inside them. Richard, the man with the revolver, was first past the bus, quickly followed by his comrade Matt carrying a katana. The weapon belonged to Nick, and unlike most of the weapons picked up by other survivors, this was an actual reproduction of the real thing. Experience had already demonstrated the usefulness of this weapon.

Nick was now at the rear of a fifteen-seat minibus. As he moved past he looked inside, checking around the seats for any sign of survivors. The strange thing was that there were no bodies or supplies anywhere near the vehicle, even the weapons were missing and that could mean only one of two things. Either the survivors stripped the vehicles and left the area or they were attacked and the convoy had been stripped. Whichever it was, there were no bodies so it looked like they must have left on foot.

He continued past the mini-bus and out into the clear area behind the vehicles. The two men were positioned next to him now. Up to the left the other two moved forwards, covering the motorway from the flank. One of these men carried a British made Lee Enfield No4 rifle, a weapon built and used originally in World War II. It used the same ammunition as the Bren and was perfect as a long-range rifle when on these kinds of tasks.

A short distance ahead was the horde, a large group of the shambling dead. Artur had underestimated, there were about forty of them and they were all heading in their direction. At this range it would take only a few minutes for them to reach Nick and his team. Richard leaned over to Nick.

"Is it me or is this all a bit weird?" he asked.

"Yeah, there's something not quite right about all this," added Matt.

Nick looked around, trying to work out what didn't fit. It didn't take long for him to spot the chains further ahead and tied to a tree at the side of the road.

"Look!" called Nick as he pointed ahead.

"I don't get it," said Richard.

"Or me, why would you have chains at the side of a main route like this? The only reason is to hold something back," said Nick.

Nick rechecked the area, looking for signs or clues that might help explain what was going on. He turned and his attention was caught by some papers on the floor of one of the recently abandoned cars. He moved forwards and pulled out the grubby stack of pages. The first sheet contained a map with several areas circled including The Green Zone, as well as the cities of Bournemouth and Reading. The second sheet was even more intriguing, it showed an inventory of people and weapons at a base in the south.

"Interesting," said Nick.

Richard, still watching the closing horde inched back to Nick to see what he'd found.

"Look, it seems these people were either heading to this place or leaving it.

"So what happened to them?" asked Richard.

Nick stuffed the papers into his pocket and rechecked the approaching zombies, they were not far away now, then it hit him.

"I know what they were doing. Look, the chains are to hold the zombies in one area. They were kept here and chained up, ready for something big," he said.

"Chained?" asked Richard.

"Oh shit!" shouted Nick as he pulled out the radio from his belt.

"Hammer One, are you receiving?" he shouted.

Richard was starting to look a little nervous. The

zombies were now only a short distance away and Nick's tone didn't inspire him with any confidence. Added to this was the first crack of a rifle, it was Jim the man with the Enfield as he started to pick off the zombies.

"Hammer One, this is an ambush. The Z-Zone is a decoy. Please respond," he said.

There was more static, punctuated by the sound of the Enfield.

"Ambush, are you sure? It all looks…" the sound from the radio cut off with a harsh screech.

Nick waved his hand in the air.

"Everybody to the trucks now, we need to get back to the convoy. Come on!" he shouted.

Matt and Richard moved back, still watching the wrecked vehicles for any sign of trouble. Nick followed them, continually checking behind with the shotgun at the ready. A grinding sound indicated one of the zombies was ripping a door out of the way. Behind it another three appeared, all heading for the group.

"There must be other groups chained up around here, we're surrounded, come on!" he cried.

Jim and his assistant were already at the bottom of the embankment and jogging along the side of the road. Every few steps Jim stopped and fired a carefully aimed shot, each time felling a zombie.

Nick went past the wrecked cars to find another two zombies lurch into view. With a double press of the dual triggers he hit them with a blast from his shotgun. The combined power of the two barrels sent the zombies flying backwards and to the ground. He didn't stop running but kept moving to the Land Rover.

The rest of their team was now past the obstructions and moving as fast as they could back to the vehicles. Right on their tails were scores of zombies, many of them appearing from the insides of some of the crashed vehicles and others from down the embankments.

Artur opened fire with the Bren, putting down heavy fire on the zombies and cutting dozens of them down. Nick and Richard reached the front of the Land Rover first, quickly followed by the rest.

"We've been screwed. This blockage was deliberate, they're hitting the convoy. We need to get back and fast!" shouted Nick, as he continued on to the driver's door.

He lifted himself up and hit the ignition, the engine instantly kicking to life. The others from the bus were now inside, all apart from Jim who was just a few feet from the door. He turned and fired another two shots from his Enfield before climbing inside. One of the passengers in the bus started firing their own roof mounted Bren gun, clearing a path to escape.

In the Land Rover Nick was revving the engine when Artur lowered himself down, shouted at Nick over the sounds of the engine and gunfire.

"I heard you on the radio, you think they've been hit?"

he asked.

"Yeah!" shouted Nick.

Nick checked around them, noting the zombies approaching in all directions. A large group was moving from the embankment and would reach the bus before it could escape. Slamming the gearstick into reverse he drove the Land Rover backwards towards the threat. The back of the vehicle was normally equipped with a spare tyre, though in these dangerous times it was now on the roof and out of harm's way. Instead, this vehicle was fitted with a simple iron spike that stuck out a foot behind the rear door. Whilst keeping his foot on the pedal Nick smashed the truck hard into the path of the group of undead. The first was skewered onto the spike and at least three were smashed against the door. The vehicle shook from the impact but a few zombies would not stop it, the four wheel drive simply drove over the bodies and smashed into the next group.

Nick slammed on the brake and came to a quick stop. Changing into first gear he forced down his foot and pushed down the accelerator. He could see that Jim had safely climbed aboard the bus and that they were already manoeuvring to move back into the middle of the road so they could head back along the motorway. The Land Rover was away first and Artur, now back on the top resumed firing at the horde. As they left the scene of the ambush he swung the gun around to face the direction they were travelling in.

"Fuck!" he shouted, banging his fist on the roof.

Nick couldn't see the problem as his view was blocked by several crashed cars. As he swerved past he saw a huge number of zombies were climbing down the embankment and making their way into the road. Nick slammed his foot down and stopped. He pulled out the radio, shouting into it whilst Artur started firing on the scores of creatures piling their way down. At this rate the road would be full and blocking their way out in less than twenty seconds.

"Hammer Two get a shift on, we've got more problems. The road is about to get hit and we need to get out of here," said Nick.

"We're on the way!" came the response.

Hammer Three was the designated weapon platform for the convoy. It carried the heaviest weapons and was the vehicle most likely to be able to fight their way out of dangerous situations. As the fire continued Nick reached behind the seat and pulled out another vintage weapon. It was a World War II Sten gun, one of the mass produced sub-machineguns used by the British. He rested it on the doorframe and added his fire to Artur's. Between them they cut down a swathe of the creatures. It was perfect timing because just a second later the bus came steaming past and straight though the channel they had created. Gunshots and shotgun blasts came from the bus as it sailed past.

Revving the engine Nick started to build up speed, attempting to catch up with the bus as fast as possible. The thumping from the Bren continued as Artur cleared any zombies that tried to get in their way. Two managed to make it into the road but the heavy iron snow plough smashed their fragile bodies and the Land Rover emerged unscathed. Putting more power down Nick moved alongside the bus and then took up the lead position.

With the zombies now well out of sight the firing stopped though their high speed continued. Nick pulled out the handset for the radio, trying desperately to reach the rest of the convoy.

"Anyone, please respond, this is Hammer Three!" he shouted, there was no response.

Pushing his foot down further the heavily laden Land Rover built up more speed and started to pull well ahead of the bus. The scene of the blocked road was now well out of view and they were only seconds from the rest of the convoy. Nick banged on the roof, Artur looked down from the hatch.

"Yes?" he asked.

"Get ready, we'll be there in twenty seconds," suggested Nick.

Artur lowered himself down and grabbed two boxes of Bren magazines and lifted them up to his firing position. Opening the tins revealed another half a dozen magazines, each one holding thirty carefully made bullets.

The two vehicles rounded a wide bend on the motorway to the sight of smoke.

"Shit!" shouted Nick.

He kept the speed up but pulled his shotgun close, making sure he was ready in case of trouble. They moved closer until they could get an idea as to what was going on. Through the large side mirrors he could see the armoured bus not far behind him. As the view of the vehicles up ahead became clearer, Nick grabbed the radio to update them on what he could see.

"We've got smoke, I think somebody hit the rest of the convoy," said Nick solemnly.

"You're kidding, right? The entire convoy?" came back on the radio.

Nick started to ease back on the power, but made sure he was still moving in case he needed to change direction in a hurry.

"Yeah. I can see five of them, all in a column, it's like they never moved. I think the sixth tried to get away, it is a bit farther back and stuck on the embankment," said Nick.

The last vehicle was smoking badly, it must have crashed or been attacked in some way.

Artur dropped back inside, looking excited.

"I can see them, look!" he cried, as he pointed ahead and past the last vehicle. Nick squinted, trying to spot whatever it was that Artur was pointing at. The motorway was full of smoke from one of the trucks and it reduced visibility considerably. He tried to look though the occasional break in the smoke to see ahead but it was too thick. Slowing down some more he became a little nervous, this could easily be an attempt to mask some kind of additional ambush. It didn't make sense though, the zombies should have finished them off at the blockade, so why would they expect them to come back?

Then, as quickly as the smoke arrived it blew to one side and revealed the remnants of the convoy. They were already moving past the first abandoned vehicle and Nick had a clear view of the ambulance that had obviously tried to reverse out of danger. A number of zombies were milling around in the middle of the road and Nick did his best to avoid them. This wasn't out of concern for them per se, more specifically he wanted to reduce the possibility of causing damage to the vehicle.

What was more interesting however, was what looked like a very dangerous security van. It was scruffy and looked like it had been modified in much the same way that their vehicles had been. Nick eased off on the power, trying to reduce the sound of the Land Rover as they moved past the rest of the convoy. He glanced sideways, noting that the cars and trucks had been looted. There was no sign of the passengers anywhere near the scene. Looking back the van was in plain sight as were a group of five men who were dragging a body out of the last car and also stripping supplies from its roof. One of the men must have spotted them though as they spun around and then ran for the van.

"Let's go!" shouted Nick as he slammed his foot down.

With a roar the Land Rover burst into life and raced down the motorway. Some of the men near the ambulance pulled out rifles and attempted to shoot at the approaching Land Rover. Bullets struck the snow plough that was fitted to the front of the Land Rover, the rounds chipped the thick steel but caused no serious damage. Artur was already in position and from his vantage point was able to put down heavy and accurate fire on them. His first burst killed two of the men and forced the rest into cover.

Nick kept his foot down till the last minute, wanting to cover the distance in as little time as possible. When he finally had to slow down he jammed down hard on the brakes. The wheels locked up and with a loud screeching sound the heavy vehicle slid to a stop, leaving two long rubber trails on the surface of the motorway. The bus was a short distance behind them but that didn't stop Nick grabbing his shotgun and tumbling out of the driver's door and into cover behind the bonnet. More bullets impacted on the reinforced bodywork of the Land Rover but none were able to penetrate the armour. He leant around the corner and was immediately forced back by gunfire from two men who were now hiding behind the van.

Artur responded with another dozen rounds fired into their direction. The loud hammering of the gun and the powerful bullets forced the men to take cover. With them pinned down Nick lurched out from cover and ran the short distance to the ambulance. One man emerged from behind it brandishing a crossbow. Without hesitating Nick pulled one trigger and then the other of the shotgun. The first shot was a little wide and just caught the man on the leg. As he stumbled and fell the second round hit him square in the chest. The round tore through the flesh and into his upper torso before he finally hit the ground gurgling blood.

Nick reached the side of the ambulance and ducked down. More fire came down on him from the two men still left taking cover behind the security van. He snapped the barrel and pulled out the two shells. The heavy fire from the Bren was deafening but Artur wasn't able to hit the men behind the reinforced armour of the van.

As Nick fed in another two shells he noticed the smoke wasn't actually coming from the vehicle but from burning foliage behind it, presumably from the previous struggle when the convoy had been hit. On the ground near him were the bodies of two people, he recognised them as the workers from the ambulance. They were neither trained nor equipped for combat, not that it mattered now.

A loud bang came from the van and it was immediately followed by a smoke trail as a flare launched up into the sky. With a red flash it ignited, sending a signal out to whoever else was waiting. Almost as though the flare was a cue the bus finally arrived and from it spilled Jim and three more men. They spread out, adding their own fire to that of Artur's, onto the van. It was now only a matter of time before they could move around the van and attack them from behind. Before they were able to get close enough though, the purpose of the flare became evident.

From above the embankment a group of motorcycles raced over the peak and down towards the ongoing battle. One of them was a large trike and carried three more men on the back, each carrying an assortment of weapons.

Jim fired three shots with his Enfield rifle, managing to take out the rider of the first bike. The bike tumbled to the ground and forced the rest of the group to spread out and move around the ambulance and van. As the bikers opened fire Nick threw himself inside the ambulance and dropped to the floor. Holes opened up all across the bodywork but luckily none of the bullets struck him. He looked out through the open door and saw a bike moving past with an outrider carrying what looked like a ball swinging from a chain. He lifted up his gun and fired a single shot into the centre of the bike. The shell knocked the passenger off and onto the ground yet but didn't take him out of the fight. More fire hit the ambulance forcing Nick back into cover.

The heavy thud of the Bren gun continued and Nick could only hope that Artur was having more success with the shooting than he was. As he considered what to do a hand grabbed at him from the front of the vehicle and started to pull him backwards. He turned to face his assailant only to find two zombies in the cab clawing at him. He fired the loaded barrel at the closest of the two, splashing its brains across the inside of the windscreen. The second reached out for his leg and in the struggle Nick flailed and kicked to get back into the rear of the ambulance.

The creature crawled over the body of the first zombie and inched towards him. From his belt he pulled out a wicked looking bowie knife and held it low and in front of him, waiting for the attack. The zombie reached out, attempting to grab at his arms. Nick easily evaded the first arm and slashed at the second, causing little damage to the already dead flesh. It moved closer and was now just a few feet away. Its mouth was contorted and its flesh pale and filthy. Cuts and abrasions on the arms showed that the creature gave no concern to its wellbeing and that it had already been through a violent second life. As it lurched forwards Nick thrust the dagger up into its throat and then pushed it up hard into the thing's brain. After months of fighting these creatures Nick was all too aware of the strengths and weakness of the undead. The blade pushed through the brain stem and then on into the back of the brain. The creature spasmed and then collapsed to the side, the dagger still embedded deeply its flesh. With a tug Nick pulled out the blade and after wiping the gore off onto the zombie's rags he replaced it on his belt. He checked his pockets before remembering he was out of shells, the rest of them were inside the Land Rover.

The sound of the motorcycles had stopped though the gun battle itself was still going on. Nick climbed into the cab of the ambulance and was pleased to see the keys were still inside. Turning the key the engine burst into life. From what he could see in the mirrors there were two men crouching behind the ambulance and still one man behind the van. Gunfire continued to come from the bus and Land Rover so they were still in the fight. With no ammunition left it seemed that the only choice he had was to run for it or try and use the ambulance. He pushed down the accelerator and then dumped the clutch, instantly applying power to the wheels. With a screech it rushed backwards towards the van and exposed the dismounted bikers to the fire from the Bren gun. He kept the power on and smashed hard into the security van. The impact threw him hard into the seat and jerked his head backwards throwing everything into darkness.

CHAPTER SEVEN

NEW SOUTH WALES, AUSTRALIA
9AM

The convoy was awake and ready to move. Normally most of the survivors were unenthusiastic about waking up and moving on, but after the disaster of the day before, everyone was keen to get going and forget it. It could not have been worse timing for morale, just after having their day off and fun games, which was now wasted. The convoy continued onwards, but the tone was now solemn and serious.

It was two hours before they reached their destination, a safe open area, ten miles from the edge of the city. This was how they operated, one RV and two trucks would raid for supplies, whilst the rest waited ten miles away in a safe location. This was not a case of a baggage train situation, but about risking the minimal necessary people and assets, whilst always having backup units to hand.

Every single vehicle in the convoy was armoured up and carried fighters, because any vehicle or person who was not in that category would not last in the Zombie Apocalypse. Bruce would normally spend this travelling time relaxing, watching movies or something similar, but not this time, his humour was lost. He sat in the front passenger seat, starring out at the endless road for the entirety of the journey, until finally called the convoy to a stop at the safe zone.

"Get two of the trucks up here, we are going in on this one," said Bruce.

Connor looked at Bruce, a little surprised. Their vehicle rarely went on raiding missions, as it was the lead vehicle.

"You sure, boss?" asked Connor.

"Yes, I need something to do, and anyway, it's probably our turn by now," said Bruce.

Connor nodded before radioing in for the two support vehicles. Bruce went to the back of the vehicle to his bedroom. The double bed en-suite room was absolute luxury in the nomadic lifestyle they had become accustomed to. He pulled open the wardrobe, revealing all of the equipment that he'd been wearing the moment the Zompoc had started. The full harness that he'd used for re-enactment was rather excessive for fighting zombies, the threats being so different for what it was intended for.

The mail protection, often referred to as chainmail, was extremely useful having large body coverage, flexibility and exceptional bite protection. However the steel armour, intended to stop blunt trauma strikes and thrusts with metal weapons, was simply unnecessary.

Bruce had quickly learnt to remove anything from his equipment which was superfluous, but never liked swapping for other items unless absolutely necessary as he was still sentimentally attached to his gear. His re-enactment armour had been treasured for years, a constant reminder of the fun he used to have.

He pulled on the stained and worn old gambeson, tying it up at the front. Five minutes later he had the plate legs and motorcycle gauntlets on, his mail shirt over the gambeson. He pulled a set of military webbing on, a simple and effective set of load bearing equipment that also carried a handgun and a machete. He felt remarkably comfortable in his old equipment that had faithfully served him through zombie combat.

The door of Road Hog flew open and Bruce stepped out onto the dusty road, the two trucks he'd requested parked next to him. He looked out towards the city, the old road signs still standing firm before them, just dirty and more faded than they used to be.

"Ok, listen up. The place we are hitting is a line of shops on a main road into the city. There's a medium size food shop, an off licence and a few other smaller establishments. There's also a supermarket between here and there on the outskirts, but it has likely been emptied long before now, but we won't rule it out completely," said Bruce.

The group of survivors formed before him were grinning, already dreaming of the delights that they were about to find.

"It's almost noon. This should be a two hour operation, potentially up to three, depending on what we find and how many places are worth stopping at. It could provide us with enough rations to last a month, so let's do it right," said Bruce.

"If it's so full of good stuff why don't we take more vehicles and people with us, get more?" asked Connor.

"Because these are the rules, we never send more than three vehicles into an unknown zone, we cannot afford to risk so much. Now mount up, it's time!" said Bruce.

A few moments later the vehicles were roaring off towards the city. Heading towards a former area of dense population was always an unnerving one. When the Zompoc began most people did their utmost to flee the large population centres, those who didn't rarely survived. Therefore, deliberately heading back into such a dangerous area was very risky. Sadly, these were the sort of risks that were necessary now because anywhere safer had been raided long before by other survivors still around.

They were approaching the area of the supermarket,

Road Hog in the centre with a truck in front and behind. From the raised position of the RV, Bruce and Dylan could already see a large pile up of cars up ahead at the junction for the supermarket. They wouldn't be able to get the vehicles within five hundred yards of the building with the huge line of cars between the crash and supermarket. Bruce picked up the radio set.

"That looks like a cluster fuck, let's head on to the next target, at least its quiet around here," said Bruce.

They drove on down the wide open road, heading ever closer to the city and reaching the suburbs where they would hope to find a fair quantity of food and drink. The streets were still lined with cars parked up as they always had been, but litter and debris were strewn everywhere. The occasional cat ran across the road, foraging for any food it could find.

The streets were empty of zombies, a surprising sight. Bruce, just like the others, wondered where the hordes of creatures had gone. This was the largest centre of population they had ever ventured near since the beginning of the zombie outbreak.

"Where do you think the zombies have gone?" asked Connor.

"I have no idea, but I doubt they've gone far," said Bruce.

"Maybe they're all home watching TV," said Dylan.

Bruce chuckled, but it was also a sad reminder of the

fact that they could never return to their homes, never relax in the knowledge that civilised society allowed them to live without fear of death every minute of every day.

They could finally see the food store up ahead.

"Connor, stop thirty feet short of the place," said Bruce.

The vehicles slowed to a stop just shy of the building. Bruce and Dylan jumped out of the vehicle with sledge hammers in hand. They walked up to it, constantly looking around for danger. There was nothing and nobody of note in sight. They reached the doors, still sealed, that was a good thing. There was nothing more disappointing in this world than to travel all the way to a food store and find it had already been emptied of everything useful. The two men brought up their hammers and smashed the door through, before walking back to the Hog.

"Take us up alongside," said Bruce.

This was their standard operation, never risk transferring supplies from shop to vehicle. Always close the distance, sealing off the area. Connor manoeuvred the vehicle just inches alongside the shop until Bruce told him to stop. They pushed the door out, it swung in through the demolished doors. Bruce looked cautiously into the shop, it being fairly dim due to the lack of lighting.

"Right, this looks good so far, grab your bags, we're going shopping," said Bruce.

The four men aboard cheered, Connor staying at the

radio to maintain communication with the others. The foragers always worked as pairs, purely for security. Bruce and Dylan headed down the far left aisle, Drake and Gordon down the far right. It quickly became clear that the shop was much larger inside than they had realised.

"Bruce, this place could keep us going for months, but we'll need hours to clear it," said Dylan.

"We may not have that long," said Bruce.

"Then get more people in here," said Dylan.

"You know what a risk that is," said Bruce.

"Yeah, and how much risk it would save us not having to do this for a while?" asked Dylan.

Bruce thought about the idea, it broke the routine, but then they rarely seemed to keep to the systems they had set up anymore. Still, the idea of being overrun after such a hard year of survival was a horrible one.

"Head back to the Hog, tell Connor to get in here and help us," said Bruce.

"That's it? Just him?" asked Dylan.

Bruce looked back at his friend, now far more serious.

"Fair enough we need extra help, but we can only use what we have, and I will not take away our lookouts. That's bloody suicidal. Now get to it!" shouted Bruce.

"Alright, no problem," said Dylan.

He jogged off down the aisle back towards the vehicle. Bruce continued on, he was walking along the lines of freezers, all had their lights off. He stopped and walked closer to one and opened the door. Before him were bags of thawed out and rotten frozen pizzas, he picked one up and simply looked at it gormlessly. The photo of the juicy hot pizza which was displayed across the cover made his mouth water, remembering the joys of convenience food. The shop truly smelt bad, but they had grown used to ignoring such smells, all he could think of was the pizza he used to order every Friday night.

Bruce dropped the box down into the freezer from where he'd got it from and carried on down the aisle. Up ahead of him he could already see the glisten of alcoholic beverages, his heart was immediately warmed. He missed a lot of the food they had to go without, but alcohol was the staple which had kept them sane. Alcohol was both a distraction from current events, as well as a reminder of the good times that everyone used to have.

As he was walking down the aisle Bruce considered his old life, the boring visit to the supermarket, his brain cell killing job, all of it now sounded so appealing after a year of desperate survival on the road.

"Bruce, Bruce!" shouted Dylan.

Bruce jumped around, expecting the worst.

"Hey, mate. This place is fucking awesome!" said Connor.

Bruce relaxed, being glad to have been surprised by the lack of the violent threat that he had expected. His friends looked so excited by the sheer quantity of food and alcohol before them. A year before, a well stocked supermarket was the most boring place a man had ever seen, but now it was more appealing than a kebab to a drunk.

"Right, well you've got twenty minutes, clear this place out!" said Bruce.

The men set on the shop like locusts, taking everything of value. The sheer quantity of canned food was enough to keep their group fed for a month or more, let alone the booze and soft drinks. Road Hog was filling up, they wished they'd brought another vehicle to stockpile supplies, but everyone understood the risks involved.

As Bruce and his crew cleared out the supermarket, Walter and Bart were sat outside in their truck, a Toyota Hilux. Walter was smoking a cigarette as the two of them sat bored in the cab of the vehicle.

"How about some music?" asked Walter.

"How many fucking times do we have to go through this? No! We're here as lookouts, anything that distracts us is a problem, is it that hard to understand?" asked Bart.

"Alright, alright," said Walter.

The two men sat for several minutes longer as Walter smoked and Bart relaxed, increasingly bored of sitting around. Bruce's raid on the supermarket was taking far longer than any raid they had ever done, and no matter what you were doing, sitting around in a truck got boring very quickly.

"Fuck this, I'm taking a piss," said Walter.

"No, stay put!" shouted Bart.

Bart grabbed at Walter's coat to stop him from getting out of the vehicle but Walter shrugged him off, opening the door and stepped outside. He slammed the door behind him, taking one last puff of his cigarette before throwing it to the ground. Walter took a large gasp of the relatively fresh air around him, and then set off around a corner to relieve himself.

"Stay in sight!" shouted Bart.

Walter didn't reply, he simply put up his middle finger as he walked away. Bart didn't know what to do. He couldn't force his partner back into the truck, nor reason with him. He sat in the driver's seat in an uncomfortable silence. A minute later a scream rang out from the direction that Walter had gone. Bart grabbed his shotgun and jumped out of the truck.

With his gun at the ready, Bart ran around the corner to see his worst fears realised. It was a long lane running between the shops, Walter was crawling towards him, a zombie holding onto his leg, and a blood trail running twenty feet back. An uncountable number of creatures were shambling towards him.

"Help me!" shouted Walter.

Bart did exactly that. He lifted his shotgun and fired directly into his friend's skull, killing him instantly. He raised the shotgun at the creature that had been attacking his friend and fired the second round, the head nearly exploded as the body was thrown to the ground.

"What a fucking idiot," said Bart.

He was kicking himself for having lost a friend, but more angry at Walter for being such a moron. Getting yourself killed in this world affected all of those around you in more than just emotional ways. He ran back to his truck and threw the empty shotgun in. Bart slammed the door and immediately picked up the radio.

"Come in all units, we have a Code Red, I repeat, Code Red!" shouted Bart.

The receiver sat unattended in the Hog, all of the survivors being inside the shop, filling their bags and trolleys with supplies.

"This is Black Dog, where the hell is Road Hog?" asked Jerry.

Jerry was on the radio in the second truck at the opposite end of the street to Bart.

"Come in Road Hog, this is Big Brewski," said Bart.

The radio remained silent.

"Bart, what the fuck do we do?" asked Jerry.

"We have no choice, there are hundreds of zombies bearing down on us, if we wait any longer we will be swamped," said Bart.

"What about Bruce and his crew?" asked Jerry.

"If they can get into the Hog they'll be fine, if they can't then it's too late for them anyway. Let's get the fuck out of here!" shouted Bart.

As he said it the horde of zombies began to pour from the street. Bart turned the engine over on his Hilux and put his foot to the floor, the wheels spinning as his vehicle lurched forward. His roo bar clipped one of the zombies as he raced down the street the way they had come. The second truck reached the horde and rammed ten of the creatures square on, knocking their speed by half as bodies were thrown aside. It was lucky they got moving when they did, as with large numbers the vehicles could be brought to a standstill.

Bruce was filling his rucksack with tins of tuna and corned beef when the little light they had began to dim. He looked down the aisle, already suspicious. He ran to the end of the aisle and his heart nearly stopped as he could see the silhouettes of countless zombies at the windows of the shop.

"Fuck! Dylan, Connor! Everyone to the Hog now!" shouted Bruce.

Connor appeared at the end of the aisle that Bruce had come from, looking at his boss in surprise.

"What's going on?" asked Connor.

"Zombies, everywhere, get everyone back now!" shouted Bruce.

He dropped the bag that he had in his hands and ran towards the door of their vehicle. The sound of the creatures beating against the glass was already getting louder, a frightening resonation. Across the shop Bruce could hear the sound of his friends shouting at each other, he could only hope they were sensible enough to know danger when they were told so.

Bruce was just ten yards from the doorway of the Hog when a window broke and cracked beside him. The security glass was breached but didn't completely disintegrate. Bruce drew his .45 Colt as the beast's hands had pulled the glass apart, with a hole already big enough for one at a time to get through. He took aim and put a round into the first creature's skull. As the first casing hit the ground, Dylan ran past Bruce.

"What the fuck is going on?" asked Dylan.

"Looks like we're getting fucked!" said Bruce.

"What do you want me to do?" asked Dylan.

"Tell me when everyone is in the Hog!" shouted Bruce.

The .45 rang out a second and third time, each a killing shot. It was hard to have anything else at this range that was a better instrument of combat. Connor ran behind Bruce as he fired his seventh and final shot. With no time to reload, he slammed the gun back into its holster and drew out his trusty machete.

"That's it boss, all aboard!" shouted Dylan.

Bruce smashed his machete down on one creature that was part the way through the hole in the glass, the heavy blade cracking the skull. He turned around and made a run for it as more of the glass was smashed apart and the horde broke through. Bruce leapt onto the Hog as Dylan yanked the door shut and slid across the three bolts. Just seconds later they could already hear their enemies beating on the door. The five men relaxed a little, Bruce sat on the floor of the vehicle.

"What the fuck just happened?" asked Connor.

"I would say it's quite clear, we just got hit by a fucking army, get on the radio and find out what the hell is going on!" shouted Bruce.

Connor looked sheepish, having left the radio to forage for supplies, but it was Dylan who was kicking himself for suggesting it.

"Big Brewski, come in, this is Road Hog, over," said Connor.

Bruce got to his feet and went to a window looking out onto the street. They were entirely surrounded by zombies already fifty deep in every direction, the numbers growing all the time. He went to the driver's seat and started up the engine. Applying power, they moved just a couple of inches and came to a halt. Bruce tried reverse, and then forwards again, they were stuck.

"We've got big problems," said Bruce.

"Come in Brewski, this is Road Hog, over," said Connor.

"This is Big Brewski, we had to bug out. There was no response from you. Walter is dead, the area is flooded! Can you get out?" said Bart.

"Negative, the horde is too large, the Hog isn't going

anywhere," said Connor.

"Are you safe for now?" asked Bart.

"Yes, all aboard and locked down," said Connor.

"Alright, sit tight, we'll think of something and get back to you. Big Brewski out," said Bart.

"So what's the plan boss?" asked Dylan.

"Nothing we can do but sit tight and hope they come up with something. The Hog can't move and we won't be able to get out of this crowd on foot," said Bruce.

"That's it? Sit and wait?" shouted Connor.

"That's right, this group has taken too many liberties with the rules recently and look where it's got us. I won't take this bullshit any longer, we're sticking to the rules we set out! Now break out the supplies, we could all do with some food and water," said Bruce.

CHAPTER EIGHT

MID-WEST, UNITED STATES

The week had finally passed, toiling of the land and the ever necessary and boring patrols. The community awoke on Saturday to the exciting thought of a ball game, something they'd only done three times since the Zombie outbreak.

Madison got out of bed and within ten minutes was dressed and out of the front door. Jack and her father were talking by Jack's truck in front of their church. She could already hear that the discussion had become heated, she walked cautiously forward.

"No, no, no, this is a day to relax and enjoy ourselves, as a community!" shouted Wells.

"Yes, and I appreciate that, but we're also burning through supplies quickly, and those supplies are becoming more and more difficult to find, taking more time and work," said Jack.

"One day will not make all the difference, surely?" asked Wells.

"Yes, it will, we're just managing at the moment, but barely, with no leeway. What happens next time we go out and find nothing? A day lost, which would be disastrous. You're suggesting we take a day off now, how is that any less disastrous?" said Jack.

"We must learn to become completely self sufficient and not have to rely on things from the old world." said Wells.

"Yes, but we haven't done that yet, have we? Until we have, I'm heading out!" shouted Jack.

"No, you're not, I order you not to!" shouted Wells.

"Order? I take orders from no man anymore. I give all my energy every day to helping this community, I'll be damned if you're going to stop me doing that!"

"Hey, hey, hey! Stop it!" shouted Madison.

Her words and presence calmed the two immediately, them both now paying her complete attention.

"That's enough, arguing is achieving nothing! Father, you want to have your game, fine, for those who can and want to. We do not own Jack, we do not pay him and he uses his own truck risking his life to support this community. Let him do what he knows best," said Madison.

Jack looked thankful, her father disapproving and

annoyed, he was already shaking his head. Wells knew he could not win this battle and must bend to their will, which he did.

"Alright, go, good luck," said Wells.

Jack and his crew of five mounted up on their four dusty and dirty trucks and fired up their engines. The vehicles rolled on by as Wells took his daughter's arm and led her into the church where no one could see or hear them.

"You just lost us a lot of discipline and structure, and made me look like a fool!" said Wells.

"I'm sorry, but I'm only doing what's best," said Madison.

"What's best? Best? You haven't a clue what's best for you, for me, for Jack or this community. We have stayed alive and free because the community has followed my command, you have no idea what you are doing!" shouted Wells.

"And you have no clue about feelings. We're human beings, we need more than a calculated existence of survival and nothing more!" added Madison.

She shrugged off her father's arm and ran out of the building. Wells was getting more and more angry, as he could already feel his hold on the community getting weaker. He may come across as a bastard to some at times, but he only ever acted in what he thought to be the best interests of the community. He was already growing to dislike this day, one that he'd allocated for fun and relief. Wells calmed his breathing and relaxed, deciding to forget his troubles and move on in the best way possible. He went outside and started preparing for the game in the field beside the church.

It was a pleasantly warm and sunny day, they went on as planned, at least most of them did, playing their games. The Pastor sat on the sidelines with the few spectators and marvelled at the community he'd managed to sustain.

* * *

The truck rumbled along the sand and dirt covered road with Jack at the wheel, his navigator, Riley, sat beside him. His '98 Dodge Ram used to be a vibrant and deep red, but it had faded significantly since it had left the factory. Much of the rough bodywork was now covered with dirt, and the front wings were dented where the bodies of zombies had met with its metal. The truck had wire fence sections bolted over all the windows, taken from the local school.

Jack kept the speed to fifty. They had a simple rule to never go above that, as they needed to drive as economically as they could. High speeds in vehicles had been the end of many of their friends in the first days of the outbreak, hitting objects such as cars, zombies, or simply just losing control in the heat of the moment.

The hunters were well equipped with protective gear and

weapons, but like the guard and patrol duties in Babylon, they could not afford to use the ammunition. Back at the base they had thousands of rounds of ammunition stored, it was regularly picked up on hunts, but all knew that it was to be kept for dire need only. In fact, the hunters specifically avoided all contact with the creatures, only fighting in self defence. The column of vehicles had been driving for four hours when Jack squinted to comprehend what he saw before him in the distance.

"Oh my fucking Christ!" shouted Jack.

"What the fuck?" shouted Riley.

The men were as shocked as each other. A mile ahead on the open plain they could see a horde of zombies, not hundreds but thousands, perhaps tens of thousands, all staggering towards them. Jack slammed the brakes on and the truck slid to a halt, the vehicles behind him braking and veering to their sides to stop. Jack opened his door and took a few steps in front of his vehicle whilst he simply looked out in astonishment. The five other men joined him, each as speechless as the other for a full minute.

"What the hell do we do?" asked Riley.

"I, I, I have no idea, we've never had to deal with odds like this!" Jack replied.

"Well they're heading straight for Babylon, what do we do? Why are there so many of them?" asked Riley.

"This is a real shit storm, let's get back to base, I'll give it some real consideration on the journey back, mount up!" said Jack.

The vehicles turned around and headed back to Babylon. The four hour drive home was an anxious one. Initially Riley tried to talk to Jack about it, but he was providing few responses, until Riley finally went quiet. For the long drive home Jack could only run all the potential actions through his head, though not finding a single one he was happy with.

It was the middle of the afternoon when the three trucks rolled back into town. The populace of Babylon was spread around, relaxing and chatting after their day of games in the heat. As Jack pulled his truck up outside the church, Wells came to the door, surprised to hear vehicles at that time of day. He hadn't expected them back for at least several more hours. Jack immediately got out of the vehicle to meet Wells, who already looked justifiably concerned.

"What's happened? What's up?" asked Wells.

"Four hours down the west road is a horde the likes none of us have ever seen. Not hundreds, but thousands, as far as we could see," said Jack.

"Doing what?" asked Wells.

"Heading straight here," said Jack.

"But how? Why so many and how do they know to head this way?" he asked.

"I have no idea, maybe it's simple coincidence, maybe they can smell us from hundreds of miles away, maybe they have group intelligence, but none of that really matters," said Jack.

"My God," said Wells.

The Pastor turned around, hiding his concern from those who could see him, simply staring up at his church. The two men were silent for a minute whilst both considered the situation.

"How long till they get here?" asked Wells.

"Well they're no more than two hundred miles away, maybe less, and assuming they average two miles an hour, we have about four days, certainly no more," said Jack.

"Will they definitely not pass us by?" asked Wells.

"It's highly unlikely, they're following the main roads right towards us," said Jack.

"Do you think you could stop them?" asked Wells.

"With every capable man and woman here, with every firearm and round of ammunition we have stored, there is a chance," said Jack.

"How would you do it?"

"Assemble about a dozen vehicles, and use them as mobile weapons platforms, matching the hordes speed and direction. The plan would work in theory, it would only be a question of do we have as many bullets as there are enemies, and could we kill them quick enough, before they reached Babylon?" said Jack.

"Alright, assemble everyone except the sentries to the trucks here, we need to share this information," said Wells.

Wells walked back into the church with a hopeless expression on his face. He stood, silently and alone, looking at the cross before him, praying in his mind for victory. Twenty minutes later the people of Babylon were gathered by the trucks and church, the intersection that had become their town's centre. Most of the crowd were still happy and content from the day of games, completely unaware of what they were about to face.

The Pastor strode out of his church to meet his invited crowd, he climbed onto the bed of Jack's truck so he could be seen and heard by all. They immediately went silent, knowing that whatever he had to say, it was clearly important.

"A half hour ago, our good friend and guardian Jack returned early with no supplies, you may all be wondering what the meaning of this is. A horde is approaching the town, the likes of which could only be gathered and guided by the Devil himself. We have perhaps four days until they reach Babylon," said Wells.

"How many are there?" asked Dale.

"It's hard to say, but thousands, maybe tens of thousands," said Jack.

The crowd gasped, astonished by the news. The survivors had managed to establish a safe and pleasant community, having thought they'd faced the worst already.

"If we'd built the walls I told you to six months ago this wouldn't have been a problem!" shouted Greg.

"None of that matters now, we can argue about the past or we can go forwards and maybe save this town!" said Wells.

"We cannot stay here. How do you expect us to fight those odds, we'll all die! We should leave while we can!" screamed Greg.

"And go where? We'll eventually face this danger anywhere we go, we've given up so much of our lives to these creatures, would you happily give up all that we have left?" asked Wells.

"What we have left is our lives, and we should like to keep it that way!" shouted Greg.

"There's a chance that we could stop them," said Wells.

"What do you suggest?" asked Dale.

"I'll have to pass you over to Jack."

Jack climbed onto the back of the truck alongside Wells, the crowd desperate to hear what amazing solution he had to the biggest threat they'd ever known.

"For the last year we've been stockpiling weapons and ammunition for use in the event of an emergency. This is the sort of emergency we were preparing for. It's hit harder than anyone could have expected, but nonetheless, we must deal with it. Perhaps we will have to run, but you should never run when you have some chance of holding onto a position as strategically important as your homes," said Jack.

"But we'll be swamped, we won't be able to kill them

fast enough!" shouted Dale.

"Not if we wait for them to come to us no, I intend to take the fight out to the bastards!" explained Jack.

"That's suicide!" said Greg.

"No, it's the safest way of fighting you can imagine. We'll fight from the backs of vehicles, always keeping the pace of the horde towards the town, never letting them get close. We'll fight using nomadic tactics. They cannot shoot back and they cannot charge. We will shoot, fire and throw everything we have got at them, and just hope we can reduce their numbers enough in the days we have," said Jack.

"And if that doesn't work?" asked Dale.

"We'll leave a number of people in Babylon, fixing up vehicles in case of evacuation, and others fortifying the town. Maybe we can't kill all of them out there, but perhaps we can kill enough that the rest can be dealt with on our own walls!" shouted Jack.

"And what then? We'll need all of the ammunition we have, a lot of the gas, more water to keep people hydrated, what will we have left?" asked Greg.

"We'll have our lives and our homes, bullets and water can be replaced!" shouted Wells.

The crowd muttered, but none spoke out any further.

"This has become a military matter now, I will leave all of the planning to Jack who has the most experience in these matters, and once he has concluded his plans, I will take charge of the work in the town," said Wells.

"Okay, here's what's going to happen. Thirty five people will be needed for the fighting, ten will handle the building of defences, five to source, repair and modify vehicles for a potential evacuation, and five for guard duties in Babylon. Those on building duty can cycle with the guards for rest. No person here can slack!" shouted Jack.

"How do we sort who does what?" asked Madison.

"You all have your own skills and talents, I expect you to make an informed decision on what you'd be best at. We need efficiency. Please volunteer for what role you would be best suited to, any that have not decided by morning will automatically be allocated. The next few days are going to be gruelling and today's been too long already. I suggest everyone has a good meal, prepares anything necessary for the morning and gets as much rest as possible," said Jack.

"Alright, that's it folks, we have a plan to get everything in order, for after today you may not have any time for anything other than for combat or evacuation! Meet in two hours for dinner. I know these are hard times, but if we stick together and work hard, we may just get through it," said Wells.

The crowd disbursed in a hail of conversation, asking more questions of each other than anyone could answer. Wells and Jack knew it was an uncertain time for the town, surviving the zombie horde was a problem they had days to solve, maintaining their morale and discipline was the first hurdle.

Later that day, those who were not on guard duty were again assembled, awaiting their evening meal. Wells, Jack and Madison were sat at a table, discussing some of the ideas that they had for the following days. Those around them were loudly discussing the matter themselves, but to no end other than pass the time, and because they couldn't stay silent.

"Madison, I want you to be in charge of finding, repairing and modifying vehicles, should we need them," said Jack.

"Why? You know I can fight, I can shoot better than most of the men here!" Madison complained.

"Yes I'm well aware of that, but I need someone capable to manage our evacuations plans. Because if evacuation becomes necessary I want it to go smoothly, I know I can trust you on that. Also, you have a good eye for what is needed, and anyone can hit those targets anyway, it's pretty hard to miss," said Jack.

"But, you need me out there!" insisted Madison.

"No, I'm relying on you back here, don't worry, you'll have your turn to fight," said Jack.

"You think the horde will reach the town?" asked Wells.

"Almost certainly, we should be able to reduce their number significantly, but the last fight will be at our doorstep. We can only hope that we're able to do enough damage to make that a situation we can deal with," said Jack.

"And what about me?" asked Wells.

"You have been our spiritual leader and manager, I suggest you maintain that position, the people need what little consistency they have left in their lives. As well as that, I'll be leading the fight, Madison the vehicles. You need to allocate someone to handle the fortifications, I suggest Greg, he's an obnoxious bastard, but capable at building. You will then be left here, in overall command of it all, the three groups with separate tasks, as well as the guard duty," said Jack

"Ok, and let us pray we do not get attacked from any other direction," said Wells.

"Indeed, that's a gamble we'll just have to take," said Jack.

"I'll need two more trucks ready for tomorrow, Dale and his brother have a couple that could work that have been laid up for a few months since we brought a ban on vehicles. I'd appreciate it if you negotiated their usage and get them gassed up before we leave in the morning," said Jack.

"No problem, I'll get on it as soon as we finish up here," said Madison.

"Also, Molotov cocktails, they could really make a difference," said Jack.

"How do we get those?" asked Wells.

"We need as many glass bottles as we can find, and enough gas to fill them, along with some motor oil. Stuff a rag through the bottle top and they're ready to go," said Jack.

"That sounds a little barbaric," Wells added.

"Yes it is, and it's exactly the sort of advantage we need in this fight. The horde is bunched up close and we'll have the advantage of fighting from safe positions, the perfect time for a Molotov," said Jack.

"Ok, I'll have a few men gather the supplies at first light and have them ready for you to oversee the finishing before you leave," said Wells.

"Do you really think you can save Babylon?" asked Madison.

"If we work together and give it everything we've got, maybe, but I can almost guarantee you that the last fight will be at our very own walls. God hope we still have them by then," said Jack.

"We will, I'll see to it," said Wells.

The town's folk finished up their meal and went to their homes to get as much sleep as they could before the days ahead. It was an uncomfortable night for most, few getting more than a couple of hour's kip all together.

CHAPTER NINE

HONOLULU, HAWAII

The small group had been on the trail for over an hour now and so far they had failed to find the runaways. The group of six wore a mixture of civilian clothes and military issue equipment and moved like a unit that had worked together many times before. Each of them men moved slowly, doing their best to avoid being spotted by their quarry.

The team had left the main perimeter of the research centre half an hour before and were walking down the empty road in the heart of one of the many abandoned districts on the island. Fuel for the power stations had run dry long ago, and with the only source of major power coming from the single remaining oil fired power station on the islands, the luxury of lighting was kept to the most populous and critical parts of the islands.

Decker, the group's leader, was an ex-army soldier who had transferred to the company three years ago. Since the outbreak he had been moved to the primary laboratory on the island of Oahu. This site was where the most critical work was being done to find ways to contain and possibly eliminate the plague that had spread worldwide.

"Sir, I think we've found one of them!" called Terry, the newest member of the group.

The rest of the men halted, looking to their leader for the order. Decker nodded to Terry as he moved forwards, checking on his finding. Ahead of them was a single storey home, it had been long abandoned and most of its windows were damaged. The door was shut though and a light trail of blood led inside. With the lighting out in this area it was difficult to get a good look inside the building. Decker pulled his night vision eyepiece over his left eye, activating its thermal mode. The building and surrounding area were cold but there was definitely heat inside.

"Got you," he whispered to himself before signalling to the group who instantly spread out, moving into positions to provide cover for the entry team.

Decker approached the door whilst Tony, a short man carrying a Mossberg M500 shotgun, moved to the other side. Tony has previously been a police officer but since the outbreak had found his time split between civilian work and assisting the security patrols on the island. He lifted the weapon up, ready for whatever waited for them on the inside.

Decker looked back, making sure the rest of the team was ready. He'd already swung his rifle behind him to his back, finding the weapon cumbersome and awkward to use in the confined spaces of a building. He lowered his hand and pulled out his stainless steel AMT Hardballer .45 automatic pistol.

With one hand on the door, and the other wrapped around the hilt of his gun, he put his hand on the handle and pulled it down gently. At the same time he put pressure on the door to try and push it open. Unsurprisingly it refused to move, that could mean only one thing, the people inside had locked the door.

Without pausing he lifted his leg and slammed his boot in hard. The door splintered near the hinges but still refused to open. He turned to Tony who emptied two shells into the approximate positions of the hinges. With one more kick the door spun open before collapsing on its last remaining, but now shredded hinge.

As the door hit the ground Tony and Decker rushed inside. Tony was in first and moved off to the left, shotgun at the ready. Decker moved to the right, his pistol kept close to his body in case anybody was waiting for him. Terry entered the doorway, holding his Bernelli Super 90 up to his shoulder. The door to the right of Decker burst open and two men rushed towards him. Even though he was surprised by the sudden arrival of the two men he was able to put three rounds into the first, the bullets slowed the man but didn't stop him. Before he could shoot anymore the second man smashed into his stomach, knocking the two of them to the floor.

Tony now had a clear view of the first man and fired two shots from his Mossberg in quick succession. The first hit the man in the centre of the torso, the second in the arm, taking it off completely from below the elbow. The power of the weapon threw the man hard against the wall before he slumped down to the ground. Tony and Terry ran over to Decker who was trying to hold off the other man.

Tony arrived first and delivered a swift kick to the man, catching him in the forehead and flying backwards to the floor. Terry followed up with more kicks, forcing the man onto his back. Decker got up, wiping the blood from his split lip. His injuries seemed minor, though he was far from impressed at being knocked down so easily.

"Tie him up," he ordered as he pointed at the man who'd nearly killed him, "is it me or are they getting stronger?"

The other two men laughed grimly as the tension from the encounter started to evaporate. This was quickly interrupted by an agitated looking Decker.

"Hold on!" he said as he looked around confused. He looked down to where the man should be. All that remained of the terribly injured man was a thick puddle of dark blood and his severed forearm.

"Where the fuck is the other one?" he shouted.

Terry looked down at the blood and Tony ran to the window, looking for any sign of the man.

"Fuck me!" said Terry, as he finished putting the restraints on his prisoner.

A series of gun shots came from outside followed by the extremely loud and unmistakable sound of a .44 magnum being fired.

"Come on!" ordered Decker as he ran for the door, his pistol at the ready.

As he left the house he found the missing man lying face down on the ground with a dozen bullet holes in his back and several more in the back of his head. About ten feet away stood a grinning Jason. In his hands he held a military issue M4 carbine, the shortened variant of the venerable M16 rifle. Stood next to him was the gung-ho hunter Joe, holding his revolver in front of him as though he was Dirty Harry himself.

"I thought you needed a hand," he said sarcastically.

Decker moved over to the body and rolled it over. The man was wearing the research laboratories own uniform.

"Huh?" said Jason as he spotted the logos.

The body was riddled with wounds, but what really caught Decker's attention was that it had a leg wound that he hadn't noticed until now. The wound was old, at least half a day and still this man was able to walk, even run.

He stood up, sighing.

"Okay, job done. Bag him, it's time to head back."

Tony and Terry stepped out, dragging their prisoner with them.

"Is it me or have we just captured another experiment?" asked Tony.

Decker nodded in agreement as he pulled out a walkie-talkie from his jacket.

"This is Decker, we've captured the runaways. Send in the trucks," he said.

A short distance away a pair of yellow headlights lit up indicating the position of their transport back. With a growl the civilian Hummer trundled towards them with another two men stood on the back. As they got closer they switched on a large searchlight that bathed the scene in artificial daylight. Decker waved them off as the light almost blinded him. The trucks pulled up past them and skidded to a stop.

"Fucking amateurs!" muttered Tony.

Decker moved up to the truck as the driver opened the door and climbed out.

"Put the body in the back and keep an eye on the prisoner," he said whilst pointing to the man still being held by his men.

The man nodded and moved to the prisoner. Decker turned back to his team whilst the others continued moving the two men.

"I think it's time we had a chat with Dr Murphy," he suggested.

The five men of his team nodded in agreement.

* * *

JOINT BASE PEARL HARBOR-HICKAM, HAWAII

Jackson and his two accomplices huddled down low to the ground to avoid being spotted. They'd left their truck several blocks away to avoid attention from the base security. Each of the men wore dark clothing to fit in with the night and pulled hooded tops over their heads. Jackson reported directly to Mr Ford, a small-time crook who had struck the jackpot in this nightmare situation.

When most people on the island had been running away, he'd built up a small and successful cadre of men who had helped him carve up a part of the city for himself. He was now a powerful man and responsible for most of the organised crime on the island since the creation of the zombie-free sanctuary. In fact the idea of the sanctuary had been a sly ruse on his part to create a population dependent on him and what he could do.

Jackson whispered to the other two.

"Ford said we need to take out the guards and the alarm system. Once they're down we send up the flare and the rest will arrive. Before we can do that though, we need to get the power down or this plan is dead in the water. Got it?" he said firmly.

The other two men nodded eagerly, though whether it was their keenness to get it over with or that they were looking forward to the operation was difficult to tell. Greg, the younger of the two men was a shifty looking, dark haired man in his mid twenties. Jonathan, the third man in the group looked much surer of himself. He carried a substantial backpack with him, as well as a scoped rifle on his shoulder. Jackson pulled out his pair of night vision binoculars and scanned the base for signs of the patrols. He picked up the sign for the Joint Base Pearl Harbor-Hickam whilst panning past the buildings. The base was a recent co-operative effort by the US Air Force and Navy. Until recently it had been packed with thousands of personnel.

Since the outbreak a year earlier, most of the personnel and naval vessels normally stationed at the joint base had been used in actions throughout the Pacific. It was normal to find a dozen destroyers, frigates and cruisers and the same number of submarines there at any one time. Now the only vessels remaining were those that had been undergoing major work or that had been abandoned in the first three weeks. Without supplies and personnel these mighty grey vessels were just lumps of steel, left to rust. The number of personnel now numbered just a few hundred, and many of these were out manning outposts on the numerous islands or guarding key buildings and ships.

Three Los Angeles class, nuclear attack submarines were tied up together. Each of them moved gently in the waters, vessels now without a role and impotent without a crew. A jetty ran from the boats to the mainland where a small barracks and several vehicles were parked. Around this area ran a tall wire fence with just one entrance, itself guarded by a three man Marines unit.

"Ok, there they are," said Jackson.

At the security point a substantial metal barrier blocked the road inside. Sitting in chairs nearby were the three Marines, each of them wearing little in the way of personal armour or protection. They were laughing and playing a game of some kind.

"You know the plan, Ford doesn't want casualties. The important thing is we need to get into the armoury. Don't forget, from our information they could have up to another five or six men inside," he said seriously.

"Are we sure the weapons are there?" asked Jonathan.

"No reason to think they aren't. The last information Ford received said all the ammunition for the flotilla and the garrison was being stored at this site. Come on, let's get started," he said, as he crept forward towards the fence.

CHAPTER TEN

ENGLAND

Nick opened his eyes but everything stayed as a blur. He shook his head and the pain hit him immediately. He closed his eyes and then opened them again slowly. Everything was dark, apart from a bright object to his right. He tried to reach out to the light but he couldn't move. Darkness replaced the light and he felt something brush past him. He started to struggle before hearing what sounded like voices. He kept still and listened, it was almost as though it was his name. He concentrated then something struck his cheek, it stung but amazingly his hearing improved a little.

"Nick, Nick, can you hear me?" asked the voice.

Once again he tried to open his eyes, the light was starting to break up into colour and it looked like he was still inside the ambulance.

"Nick?" came the voice, it was now starting to sound like Artur.

With a final shake of his head the view started to improve and he could see the inside of the ambulance. To his right Artur was cutting at the seatbelt that he must have put on during the struggle. Moving his head over to the left his attention was brought to the scene through the cracked windscreen. There were two motorcycles and a trike along with several bodies nearby. What looked like Jim and one other were walking along, checking the bikes, probably for ammunition or supplies. Off to his left was the Land Rover, and at the side was the bus though it looked like it had taken some damage in the battle.

Artur loomed up close to his face.

"Nick, are you okay? We have a problem," he said.

There was a ripping sound and Nick was finally free of the belt. Artur helped him up and out of the vehicle. Nick looked around at the scene of the battle. There were bullet casings and blood all around as well as a good many more bodies than he would have expected.

"Problem?" asked Nick. "Where did all these bodies come from?"

"Okay, actually we have several problems," said Artur with a grin.

Nick was still feeling a little light headed and his hand reached out to the ambulance to steady himself.

"Where are the bikers?" he asked.

"Dead," answered Artur, "well, apart from the one we captured."

"Captured?" asked Nick.

"Yeah, the fight was pretty much over after you crashed your ambulance here into their van. The last guy tried to get away on his bike. Jim shot him in the shoulder and he crashed over there," said Artur, as he pointed out into the distance.

Nick was feeling much better already and was glad to take a few gulps of water from Richard when he appeared.

"You feeling a bit better? Some nice moves there!" he said.

Nick tried to smile.

"Any news on the rest of the convoy?" asked Nick.

Artur looked solemn and then waved over to Jim who joined them at the ambulance.

"Good to see you back, thought we'd lost you for a while there," he said.

Jim took pad of paper from his jacket and handed it over to Nick. It was small and the cover was folded back to reveal hastily written details of some kind of camp.

"What is this?" asked Nick.

"We've been getting information out of our prisoner for the last twenty minutes. It looks like they've set up a raiding camp nearby, just off the motorway. They're vultures, feeding off travellers on the main routes," he said with a disgusted tone to his voice.

Nick examined the pages in detail. The first page showed the motorway and a series of roads leading to an area described as the camp. He turned the page to find a list of vehicles and numbers.

"Holy shit, you got this from the prisoner?" he asked.

Jim nodded in acknowledgement. Looking back at the pad Nick was astounded at how large the operations were that these people were running.

"It says here they have over forty prisoners including our people. It also says they have over fifty people, all armed?" asked Nick.

"That's what he says," said Jim.

"Why are they taking prisoners?" asked Nick.

"I don't know. They do have two buses though on the inventory lists. Maybe they're slavers?" asked Richard

"Slavers? Raiders? You believe this shit?" asked Nick.

Jim and Artur both shrugged then Artur spoke.

"There's more, a lot more. They've been using the zombies as their foot soldiers, that's why they've been so successful."

Jim interrupted, "Look, they're using the things to drive people into ambush zones. Remember we heard about that compound near Stroud getting wiped out last month?" Nick nodded.

"Well, they used the zombies to attack the place then picked off the survivors when they tried to escape. The prisoner says he was one of the people in the compound that was caught," said Jim.

"Bullshit!" said Nick. "Where is he?" he asked.

Richard pointed to the armoured bus near the Land Rover. With an effort Nick pushed himself up and staggered over to it with Richard going with him. The prisoner was tied up in the back of the bus being carefully watched by one of the passengers. Nick moved up closely, examining the man. He wore the typical biker gear, gloves, jacket and trousers plus the over sized leather boots. He didn't look like a biker though.

"What's your name?" asked Nick.

The man looked terrified, he fidgeted with the ropes but they were tied down firmly. Nick picked one of the food bags and swiped it across the man's face.

"I asked you a question!" he shouted.

"Jenkins! Don't hurt me!" the man stuttered.

Why did you attack our convoy? We've got enough problems in the Zompoc without you adding to them. Why?" he shouted.

"I didn't have a choice. We were told we either joined up with them or we would be made to join the zombies," he continued.

"Rubbish, why would they let a zombie get to you?" said Nick.

The man shrugged, ignoring the question. Nick raised his hand as though to strike again.

"Okay, okay. Look, they use the zombies to help them attack towns for supplies. Anybody they can't feed or use for their raids they turn into a zombie and then use them anyway," he said.

"What do you mean, turn?" asked Nick.

"They put…they put you in a cage with zombies and let them attack you. They made us watch it happen. In the end you turn and you're one of them," he muttered.

Nick stepped back, looking at Richard.

"Do you believe this shit?" he asked.

Richard shrugged and then pulled out a map from his pocket. He showed it to Nick. It was the route that they sometimes used for their convoy runs to the north of the country. Along the main motorway, a good distance north of Manchester, was a series of villages and towns that were circled in red. They were all in a similar area of no more than fifty square miles.

"These are all areas we've lost contact with over the last year. What this man has told us confirms that this group has raided and destroyed five compounds and villages near Lancaster in the last three months. They're making their way south, look," said Richard as he pointed to the map.

Nick looked carefully. Though they rarely travelled that far north anymore, it was still worryingly close to their own safe areas if these people kept moving south.

"If this is true, then why are they so far from home?" he asked.

Before Richard could speak the prisoner answered.

"Food. Plain and simple. They don't make anything, they take what they need and move on. From what I've worked out they started near Glasgow but were forced out of the city. They've been growing in numbers and ransacking towns all the way south on the main roads. They sent a small group of us to set up here to watch the east and west routes for people and supplies, and to see if it's worth coming down this far south," he said.

How long have they been doing this?" Nick asked.

"About three months now, that's what the guys told me anyway."

"How do you communicate with the rest of them then if you are so far away?" asked Nick.

"The old army truck has a radio in it, we use it once a day with updates," said the prisoner.

Nick climbed back out of the vehicle and faced Richard whilst he thought for a moment. Richard spoke first.

"What do you think?" he asked.

"Well, our first job is to try and rescue those people, the second is to get back to the Green Zone and fast," said Nick.

Richard nodded in agreement as the two of them walked back to the Land Rover. The rest were still loading weapons and supplies into their two vehicles. Nick unfolded his map onto the bonnet of the Land Rover and made some notes. After a few seconds he leaned back, deep in thought and then looked up to the sky, noting that it was already starting to darken.

"Shit!" he muttered as he turned to Richard.

"Get everybody here, I've got a plan and we need to move fast," he said.

* * *

Nick steered the large trike as he pulled off the main road. The large number of lights proved their worth as with no streetlights the route would have been impossible to navigate at this time of night. As he turned the bend he could see the fires of a large encampment up ahead, it was exactly as Jenkins had described it. The site was an old service station with ample space for people and vehicles. He turned around and gave a signal to the three men hanging onto the back who in turn flashed red torches at the Land Rover and bus following them.

The trike continued forwards until met by the first of three guards patrolling the outer perimeter. The men signalled for him to slow down which he did. As he approached they recognised the trike and waved him on through. They were obviously more interested in looking out for the undead than the living. This was probably a good idea on most nights, not this one though.

"So far so good," whispered Nick to Richard who was holding on to the frame right behind him.

Nick maintained his speed and rode straight into the camp, noting that little attention was given to him, probably because they were all too familiar with the bizarre and over the top contraption. The vehicles following slowed down and waited ready at their allotted location.

Nick whispered over to the three on the back.

"Remember, we hit the truck first then the tyres of the rest of their vehicles. After that the zombies and the very last job are the prisoners. Got it?" he said.

The men on the back nodded in acknowledgment. Each wore the garb of the bikers that had been recently killed in the battle on the motorway. Providing they didn't get too close they should be okay. Nick moved on past the fires and pulled up alongside the rest of the motorcycles. He switched the engine off and was pleased to hear the loud noise of heavy metal music and laughter from the campsite. The more noise the easier it would be for what they had to do.

The truck was easy to spot. It was the largest vehicle, apart from the two buses. He walked towards it with the other three men following a short distance behind. Nick counted a dozen bikes, the truck, two buses and a dozen heavily modified pickup trucks and cars.

At the end of the line of vehicles was the first bus, it was being guarded by two men, each armed with rifles. Richard spotted something ahead and gave a signal, the four moved quickly to the side of the nearest truck.

"Five minutes then meet at the last truck to deal with the guards. Ready?" asked Nick.

With a nod the group split up for their tasks, the Johnson brothers heading over to the motorcycles and vehicles whilst Richard followed Nick to the buses. With the first two gone, Nick moved to step back into the open when another man stepped out in front of him, stopping him in his tracks. The man looked dazed and confused to see Nick.

"Hey, man, where's Rollo?" said the man in a drunken slur.

"In a ditch!" answered Nick as he smashed his fist into the man's face and then dragged him off behind the vehicle.

With the man on the ground he followed up with a few kicks just to be sure. Richard caught up with him and moved closer in case of trouble. He looked down to check the man on the ground then back to Nick.

"Yeah, he's out, we okay?" he asked.

Nick nodded, "Come on!"

Leaving the man on the ground they continued towards the truck. It was a large Mercedes built four-wheel drive vehicle known as a Unimog. Nick and Richard climbed up into the cab whilst the others continued their work on the other vehicles. Inside the cab there was no sign of keys but the radio was a substantial unit and easily found in the centre of the console.

"Can we take the radio, it could be useful?" asked Richard.

"Look at the thing, it's military spec and the cables run into the unit in the back. We'd need to take the whole truck. We don't have the time for this, just disable everything you can," said Nick.

Nick pulled out the tools he'd brought whilst Richard ripped apart all the electronics he could find. With the tip of a screwdriver Nick jammed it into the front of the radio set and prized off the panel. With the delicate circuits exposed he pulled and stabbed at every part he could find. In just seconds the radio was ruined.

"Come on, let's go," said Nick as he jumped out of the vehicle.

Outside the Johnson brothers had done their job on as many of the vehicles as they could reach. Following Nick they inched slowly towards the end of the column where the two buses were parked. Off to their left were the camp fires and the raiders listening to their music and drinking with abandon. To the right were the last two trucks forming a barrier to the motorcycles on the other side. Ahead of them, but in front of the buses, were four containers, each one large enough to fill the back of a large truck.

"That's what Jenkins said they would be like, right?" asked Richard.

Nick nodded and then lowered himself as he considered

the next, critical part of the plan.

"It's important we cause the confusion now or we'll never get them all out. Okay?" he asked.

The younger of the Johnson brothers spoke, "Are you sure there's no other way?"

Nick shrugged, "If you can think of one tell me. Right now we need to use their strategy against them. Look on the bright side. Ultimately we'll be doing everybody a favour."

With a look of resignation they agreed. Nick jabbed his thumb towards the first bus and they fanned out, each moving into position. The Johnson brothers moved straight to the containers and knocked out the bolts holding the hatches shut. As soon as they were opened hands reached out.

"Fuck me!" shouted the younger brother as he jumped back from the creatures.

With the din from the loud music nobody could hear him and more importantly, nobody was looking out for zombies inside the encampment. In seconds they had the hatches to the rest of the containers opened and ran back to join Nick and Richard in their position ready to storm the buses.

"Is it done?" asked Nick.

The two men nodded.

"Okay then, let's do this!" said Nick, as he pulled out a small pistol crossbow from his jacket and put it into its ready position.

The other three pulled out similar weapons and did the same. The weapon might be small, but with a good shot it could place a steel bolt into a man's head. Checking from side to side he could see the other three were ready. He turned back and then pulled the trigger. With a dull twang the bolt released and smacked into a guard's throat. It was lower than he intended but it had the desired effect. The guard fell to the floor, grabbing at his bleeding wound. Two more bolts struck his comrade, one in the shoulder and the other in the forehead, killing the man instantly.

Richard moved ahead and pulled open the door to check inside. A man was sitting in the driver's seat brandishing a sawn off shotgun. With a roar he pulled the trigger and emptied both barrels into Richard's chest. The close range blast sent him back a dozen feet before he landed on his back, killed instantly by the blast. Pulling one of the captured Colt 1911s from inside his jacket Nick put four bullets into the man before jumping inside. The other two men ran past and on to the next bus.

Nick spotted the keys on the man's belt and pulled them off before dragging the dead man out of the driving seat. Before he could finish a woman tried to grab at him, probably thinking he was one of these thugs. He pushed her back but in seconds the bus was alive with activity. Though the passengers were all awake they were obviously terrified and had said or done nothing so far.

Nick turned around to face the passengers.

"We're here to help you. Keep quiet and keep your heads down. Are there any other prisoners here?" he shouted.

Some of the passengers kept talking but one was a gunner from their own convoy. He shouted out to Nick.

"Nick, it's me, Carter!" he called.

Nick signalled for him to come to the front.

"There were three others, they took them to the other bus about an hour ago. That's it," he said.

"Glad to see you. How about our people, how many of you made it?" asked Nick.

"Only eleven, they shot some of us on the way here!" he shouted.

"Fuck!" muttered Nick.

He reached inside his jacket and pulled out another pistol and handed it to the man, indicating to the window on the left. The young man moved to the window, watching for trouble. The Johnson brothers were already back and climbed inside the bus.

"Just bodies on the bus, they all had their throats cut, there's some sick shit going on here," said the younger of the two.

The older Johnson smacked his little brother on the head.

"Watch your language!" he said before turning back to Nick. "Where's Richard?"

"Dead," he replied.

A bright flash lit up the area followed by a series of gun blasts. This was quickly followed by the sound of shouting and more gunfire.

"Good job," said Nick, "come on, we haven't got much time, we need to go."

Pushing the key into the ignition Nick twisted the key and for a moment his heart nearly stopped, nothing happened. He pulled out the key and then tried again, with a shudder the engine started and the interior lights all lit up. Nick revved the engine and then hit the lights switch, instantly lighting up the campsite and revealing the swirling melee of bikers, men and zombies. There were people on the ground and the zombies seemed to be getting the upper hand already.

"Do it!" shouted Nick.

The older Johnson pulled out a squat looking pistol and held it out of the closest open window. With a blast it fired upwards, leaving a bright red trail behind. Nick put down the power and the bus started to move slowly forwards.

Holes appeared in the windscreen as the raiders attempted to halt their progress, but the fire was sporadic and poorly aimed.

"They'd better get here fast," shouted Nick as he floored the accelerator and turned towards the entrance and a number of armed guards.

The bus was heavily loaded down with people and took quite some time to pick up speed. More bullets struck the glass and a few made it inside, hitting the passengers. Some started to shout and at least one started screaming. Carter and the brothers opened their nearest windows and returned fire as best they could.

Several bright lights lit up ahead and then flashes from a large number of weapons erupted. No bullets struck the bus though and it rushed out of the entrance unscathed. As they moved past the outer guard post Nick spotted their own armoured bus and Land Rover bristling with men and weapons. Their fire was overwhelming and it dealt with the immediate threat of the raiders giving chase. As the bus continued off down the road the other two vehicles turned and followed, all three heading for the opposite motorway exit that would allow them to avoid the roadblocks set by the raiders. It took just two minutes for their small convoy to reach the motorway and the open road.

Nick pulled out the radio he'd been carrying.

"Why didn't you use it earlier?" asked the younger brother.

"Simple really, the raiders are well equipped and these radios are just normal short range CB sets. They're easy to listen in on with any other CB equipment. We couldn't take the chance. Now we're on the road the risk is worth it," said Nick.

"This is Rescue One, we all good?" he asked on the radio.

"Good to hear you, man. Yeah we're all good here. Did you get them all?" asked Jim in the armoured bus.

"Yeah, all that were left. Any sign of pursuit?" asked Nick.

There was a silence for a short while.

"Looks clear at the moment, give it time though, those bastards won't let this lie."

Nick nodded as he placed the radio on the dashboard.

Carter moved up to the front of the bus to speak with Nick.

"What's the plan?" he asked.

"We're going to get to the Green Zone asap," answered Nick.

There was a scream from the back of the bus. Nick looked in the large mirror but couldn't quite see what was happening.

"Carter!" he shouted, "take over!"

The young man grabbed the wheel and then slid into position as Nick moved. The bus lurched a little to the left and then continued on its straight path. Nick moved down the bus and past the scared looking people. There was a struggle at the back. He pushed past them until he was just a few feet from the rear. Two men were holding down a woman and the other passengers were shouting and trying to get away.

"She's infected, look!" shouted the taller of the two men.

Nick looked closely, the woman did have the tell tale signs of a bite, she was pale and already biting and grabbing at the two men. Either she had turned or soon would. In a year of survival in the Zompoc Nick knew that once bitten you never survived, it was just a matter of time before you turned.

"Everybody move back!" Nick shouted as he waved to the front of the bus.

Nobody moved. Most of them were too stunned to do anything.

Nick pointed the gun at the roof and fired a single shot.

"Move! Now!" he shouted, this time they listened.

As the group cleared just the two men and the pinned woman remained. Nick stepped forward and hit the emergency open lever on the rear door. With a hiss it swung open to reveal the blackness outside. The two men grabbed the struggling woman and dragged her to the door. Though slight in build she held on with surprising strength. Nick held out his shotgun, placing it just a foot in front of her chest. The woman showed no concern and simply growled at the muzzle.

"Now!" shouted Nick and the two men jumped away from the woman.

Without hesitating Nick pulled the triggers and put two shells into her chest, blasting her into the motorway and into the darkness. He turned back and returned to the front of the bus, noting the groans and complaints from what they probably thought was excess force in his part.

From out of the windscreen he noted the armoured Land River overtake them and then take up position in front of the bus. Nick turned back to the passengers, signalling with his hand that they needed to listen.

"I know you've had a bad time, things are about to get better though. We're heading for the Green Zone. For those of you who haven't heard of it you'll be pleasantly surprised."

A man stood up, shouting Nick down.

"What if we don't want to come with you? What if you're no better than those raider bastards?" he asked angrily.

"It's up to you. If you want to stay just say so and we'll let you out," he gestured to the front door.

A young woman at the front waved to get his attention.

"What is the Green Zone?" she asked.

"We set up the Zone over three months ago as a safe area. We have food, clothing, weapons and you can get back to some kind of a life. I suggest you all get some rest, it will be a few hours before we get there and who knows what we'll run into on the way," he said.

Nick slumped down into the front seat, opposite the driver and for the first time in over six hours closed his eyes.

The much depleted convoy continued down the motorway, towards the Green Zone and to safety.

CHAPTER ELEVEN

ENGLAND

Dave drove out with the usual crowd, some of the idiots who had put them in such a sticky situation the day before. Only one of the fools, Richard stayed behind. He said he was feeling the effects of a cold. Each team of 'collectors' was six men, four needed for missions, a further two were substitutes and spare men enabling them to cycle people, accounting for illness and exhaustion. The group went on, Dave, Tommy, and the other two idiots from the day before. The task today was to raid a petrol station seventy miles away, but safely on an A-road miles from any major populace centre.

It was a hot day, too hot to be stuck inside a Land Rover with very few ventilation areas and no cooling. All the windows were covered with wire mesh and bars, restricting the little airflow they could get into the vehicle. The vents running beneath the windscreen could no longer open, restricted by the windscreen protection they had fitted. Luxuries were something they were becoming used to living without, but not quickly or easily.

It took the group two hours to reach the service station, going along small roads and keeping engine revs low to conserve fuel. They arrived to the pleasant sight of an abandoned area. In life before the Zompoc a desolate location was a depressing one, but now it signified the kind of safety they desired.

It was a small village petrol station with a shop that was smaller than most children's bedrooms. Someone has clearly grabbed a few bags from this place before, but quite some time ago considering the dust build up on the empty shelves. Many months ago, people would just take what they needed short term, or as much as they could fit in a rucksack. The more prepared and well organised survivors that had made it through the first year knew to never leave anything behind, unless it risked death or infection to a group member.

Dave's system revolved around his standard group of four people and two vehicles. The drivers stayed at the wheels of their trucks, parked at opposite ends of the location, whilst the two navigators would raid for supplies. In an ideal world, he would always have wanted six people for such a mission, but lives were simply too valuable to risk.

The two navigators in this situation, Tommy and Dave, each carried a large army Bergen on their backs, and pulled along big wheeled bags behind them. Both men carried a club hammer, the default and easily findable weapon for all members of the group. These were carried on lines attached to their belts. They also carried a few small bladed weapons, both for utility and backup defence.

The small refrigerator that used to carry sandwiches and other savoury snacks was completely empty. The shelves of chocolate bars and crisps were only mildly depleted. The two men began stuffing their bags with supplies.

"Oh, yeah!" shouted Tommy.

Dave looked around to see what had got Tommy so excited, a shelf of corned beef, tinned hot dogs and beans. These were the kind of luxuries to get excited about in the world they lived in today. It was just a small shop, but it was a trip well worth making. Dave leapt behind the cashier's desk. A large amount of tobacco and alcohol had been taken, but there was still plenty left. The cash register was open and empty. This place had obviously been done over soon after the Zompoc had begun, before people realised quite what an apocalyptic scenario they were facing.

In just a matter of two minutes they had filled their bags with everything worth taking from the shop. They threw the bags back into the vehicles. Clearly this station still had plenty of fuel in it, but they were well stocked back at Everglade for now, having copious amounts of red diesel stashed from all the local farms. Dave looked out down the small street where about a hundred yards away a solitary zombie was staggering towards them.

"Let's kill that fucker!" shouted Tommy.

Tommy jumped onto the side of the Land Rover, waving his driver on. The vehicle lurched forward and raced towards the single beast. Tommy, hanging on with one hand on the galvanised roof rack, drew his club hammer from his belt. As the vehicle stormed past the creature Tommy swung the hammer into the zombie's face, the speed and force sending it tumbling off its feet and into the air. The creature slammed quickly down to the tarmac, its face demolished by the blow. The vehicle turned around and pulled up alongside Dave who was stood next to his vehicle.

"You see that? Fucking beautiful!" said Tommy.

"You're an idiot," said Dave.

"We have to start mopping up sometime," said Tommy.

"Not for killing it you idiot, but for being so reckless," said Dave.

"Just having some fun, you should try it sometime," said Tommy.

"Look, there are hundreds of thousands, maybe millions of those creatures in this country alone, and just a handful of us. One accident is more than we can afford, so start acting with some god damn sense!" shouted Dave.

"Alright, alright, we going then?" asked Tommy.

"Yep, load up, we're done here, time to go back and maybe enjoy some of this," said Dave,

"Mmm, sausages!" said Tommy.

Dave grinned as he got back into his vehicle. Tommy was a reckless fool, but one could not afford to be picky about choosing their friends in this day and age. The vehicles trundled on back to the compound. It was a long and boring journey, though the day was already beginning to cool slightly by the time they reached sight of Everglade. It was the same place they had left earlier in the day. So many of them were forced to simply keep running and stay on the move after the Zompoc had begun. The chance to have a home to return to or stay in each and every day was a luxury they all appreciated.

It was already well into the afternoon when the vehicles came to a halt within the walls of the compound. Roger was there to welcome them as ever, to review their day's haul and assess any problems.

The work day was over for them now. Roger had a number of the survivors working the land in an attempt to grow their own food. This was only recently started and would take time until they could see any results. It was quite clear to all of them that scavenging from remnants of the old civilised world that they used to know would go on for some time to come.

Dave went to bed that night, content in the knowledge that the status quo had been maintained, and that they were now in a better position than they'd been at the beginning of the week. Sadly, he had no idea what disaster was about to ensue. Richard, who had been ill after their rescue attempt, had deteriorated in his own bed. No one had checked on him, having been so annoyed at him for his foolish activities. Nobody had considered the possibility of infection from the rescue at the supermarket.

The close proximity with such large numbers of creatures could easily have infected several of them, but the elation of everyone being rescued had made them all throw caution to the wind and forget all of their sensibilities and concerns.

Dave was awoken by the sound of screams, never a pleasant sound, but especially when you knew they were more likely a result of zombies than domestic violence. He was still mostly dressed, as everyone stayed at least partly ready to move at all times in the zombie infested world they'd come to know. He pulled his boots on and picked up his club hammer. He ran out of the room to find Graham stood in the corridor, looking down it, but too scared to move.

They were on the second and top floor of the house, the screams were from the first floor. Tommy joined Dave's side and Roger came rushing out of his bedroom, shotgun in hand. The double barrel shotgun was the only firearm they had in the group, a personal item Roger had owned since long before the Zompoc. Sadly, he only had a handful of shells left for it, using most of them to save his skin in the first weeks of the outbreak. One of the women, Sandra, came running up the stairs.

"Help, help!" she shouted.

"What is it?" asked Roger.

"Zombies, they're in the building!" she screamed.

"Are you sure?" Roger asked.

"Yes, I saw Richard and Scott, they were already turned. I couldn't see how many more, but most of the floor," said Sandra.

"Shit!" shouted Roger.

Before they could think any more one of the zombies was nearing the top of the stairs. Roger shouldered his shotgun and fired off a round, the scatter shot obliterating the creature's head. The creature was Scott, one of their friends until a few hours before, a man who had survived a year in this horrible world.

The screaming and sounds of fear and pain got louder as more and more of the building was being consumed. They had never had much of a plan in place for this sort of situation, as they'd only protected themselves from the outside world.

"How the hell could this have happened?" asked Dave.

"Somebody must have got infected, it's the only way," said Roger.

"But how?" asked Graham.

"After Tommy's fuck up the other day, who knows," said Roger.

Before they could carry on the conversation the sound of an engine roaring to life outside got their attention. They ran to a side window in the hallway to look out. The Land Rover Discovery was roaring towards the gates with no intention of stopping.

"That's my truck!" shouted Graham.

The armoured vehicle smashed through the gates, knocking them both off their hinges. It was a dire sight for the survivors that now stood together. Somebody had obviously been selfish enough to bolt at the first sight of danger, with no consideration for their fellow survivors. Had that not happened, there was a chance of again purifying the complex, but not now. With the gates down and a substantial number of creatures amongst them, anything could happen in the time it would take to fully clean up.

"What do we do?" asked Dave.

"As much as this is our home, it is now too dangerous to stay here. Even if we could win the fight, the risk of infection is too great and not just from these creatures, but any that could flood through the gates, as well as infectious material now scattered through the complex," said Roger.

"But what about everything we've built here?" asked

Graham.

"It is irrelevant, all that matters is us, the survivors. Buildings can be replaced, there are certainly enough vacant ones around now," said Roger.

"Right, then we need a way out," said Dave.

"We have to get out of here in the shortest route and time possible, with little fighting," said Roger.

"Then we'll take the stairs right to the hallway and straight to the vehicles," said Dave.

"Hopefully with all the confusion of those infected that are still fighting we stand a chance of getting out," said Roger.

"Tommy, Graham, Dave, grab any gear you have and meet me back here," said Roger.

"What about the others?" asked Dave.

"What others?" Roger asked.

"The rest of the survivors here, they're our friends and family," said Dave.

"Not anymore, those lucky and capable enough will make their way out like us. Those that don't are nothing more than zombies, condemned to the same fate as all the other poor bastards before them," said Roger.

"Fuck, fuck, fuck!" shouted Dave.

"This is bullshit," said Tommy.

Roger grabbed Tommy by his shirt and pulled him in close.

"Look you moron, you've brought this shit upon us by

breaking the simple rules we lived by, so I don't want to hear anymore of your crap!" shouted Roger.

"Okay, guys. Chill out, this isn't the time," said Dave.

Roger let go of Tommy and shoved him away.

"Indeed, we have to take stock of what we have. We are at least all still alive and uninfected, let's keep it that way. Now grab your kit and get ready to move," said Roger.

Graham, Dave and Tommy each strapped on all of their personal armour and weapons as quickly as they could. Dave was pulling his leg armour on when a second shotgun shot rang out from the corridor. He stumbled out of the bedroom with the rest of his kit in hand. Roger has taken the life of another creature. Dave continued to pull on his equipment in the hallway as Roger reloaded his shotgun.

"How many rounds you got for that?" asked Dave.

"These are the last two unfortunately," said Roger.

"That sucks," said Dave.

"Indeed," said Roger.

"Have you got any other weapons?" asked Dave.

Roger turned to reveal a military sabre hanging from his belt.

"I've got this," said Roger.

Dave knew well that it wasn't a weapon well suited to their task, but it's what he had, and at least he felt safe with it. Experience had taught all of them that most swords were not particularly well suited to zombie slaying. The blades required great skill to use effectively, were prone to damage, and often difficult to use in many of the spaces they fought in.

"What can I do?" asked Sandra.

"Can you fight?" asked Roger.

"I made it this far didn't I?" said Sandra.

"Dave, grab her a weapon," said Roger.

Dave went into his bedroom and came back out with a hammer, the typical household type. He kept it as a spare weapon beside his bed and as a general tool. He passed it to her, it would be far better suited to her than the bulky and heavy club hammers he liked to use.

"Everyone ready?" asked Roger.

The group nodded.

"Now remember, there are likely ten or more zombies in the building, potentially more since the gates were smashed, these are not our friends anymore, even though they may look like them. Dave, you lead the way, get us to the trucks as quickly as you can," said Roger.

"Alright people, let's move!" shouted Dave.

They headed off along the corridor, none of them wanting to journey down the stairs. This kind of pressure and stress was something none of them had experienced or endured since the first months of the Zompoc. The supply runs were so carefully considered and planned that none of the men having to do them ever had to face such a dangerous situation. Now, after all their months of work and effort the entire complex had been compromised by one stupid decision, one man who could not follow the simple and careful rules that Roger had laid out.

They reached the top of the stairs. The screams were lesser now, with perhaps only one person still making noise in the building. That suggested that the entire two floors below them were now hostile. All that Roger and Dave could now think was how much more care they would put into internal security could they go back and do it differently. They were already planning in their heads how they would set up the next complex. The possibility of not making it out of the building never crossed their minds. After a year of survival, the possibility of failure and death was never something that they gave a moment's thought.

This group of five survivors now had the raw determination and drive that any who survived had experienced in the opening days of the Zompoc, the raw survival instinct. It was this single track mindedness and ability to act that had allowed all of these people to remain alive. They were hardened veterans of the Zombie Apocalypse, and nothing would stop them.

Dave led the way down the first flight of stairs at a steady pace, they all knew the importance of getting out as quickly as possible. They made it down the first flight of stairs to the hallway of the first floor of the house. A zombie was already tumbling towards them, but not blocking their path to the next floor.

"Tommy, lead them on, I'll deal with this," said Dave.

The survivors moved past Dave. He knew that any creatures this close to them must be dealt with, as any holdup on the ground floor could lead them to fighting on all sides. He moved towards the creature, doing his best to ignore the fact that he had spoken to the man just the day before. He lifted the hammer up to his side before smashing it into the creature. The thick flat head of the tool crushed into the beast's jaw, breaking it from the skull and sending the body tumbling against the radiator on the wall. Not risking a comeback from the creature, he swung again, hitting the back of the head. The zombie's head was resting on the radiator, the hammer crushing the skull nearly flat to the metalwork. Blood sprayed up the wall as the body slumped down the wall to the floor.

Dave followed on down the stairs after his fellow survivors. He reached them at the bottom where they stood, mortified. Through the corridor to the kitchen they could see four of their former friends, all with blood dripping from various wounds and the crazy expression in their eyes that they had come to loathe and fear. The path to the front door, which was wide open, was block by another two creatures. Roger held up his shotgun, he fired his first round, scattering blood and brain matter across the hall. He quickly aimed at the next one and pulled the second trigger on his weapon. The scattershot was off centre and tore flesh from the side of the beast's face, leaving blood trailing down its clothing, but it wasn't dead.

Roger drew his sword from his side and walked quickly towards the creature, he swung at the beast as if the sword was a hammer. The clumsy strike missed the head and imbedded in the collar bone. The zombie's jaw opened and hissed at Roger, the wounds not having any major effect on it.

"Out of the way!" shouted Dave.

He ran forwards and without stopping smashed his hammer into the creature's forehead, cracking the skull open. The force of the blow sent it face down to the floor. He looked around. The zombies in the kitchen were already staggering towards them.

"Let's move, people!" shouted Dave.

The group began moving towards the door with Dave at the lead, but they were stopped by a creature that walked into the doorway before them. Dave stopped immediately as he recognised the hair and body outline he was so familiar with, Kailey. He stood, speechless, having to kill his friends was not new to him, but this was different. For every month he'd lived in Everglade the knowledge that every time he went out into the infected lands he could return to see her face had kept him going. This was the end of hope for Dave, what was there to live for?

"What are you waiting for?" shouted Roger.

Dave stayed silent, his mouth was dry and his hope was

lost.

"Fucking do it and we can get out of here!" shouted Tommy.

"I, I can't," said Dave.

The body of what used to be the woman he loved so much began shambling towards him, now just a few feet away. His hammer was still at his side, arms and shoulders hunched. Dave had lost all sense of priority, shocked by this one last loss that pushed him over the edge.

"Get out the fucking way!" shouted Tommy.

He pushed Dave aside and ran at Kailey, immediately bring his hammer down onto her cranium. The skull split and blood seeped out, mingling with her blond hair and pouring onto her blouse. Dave watched in horror as her body swayed until it finally toppled to the floor. Tommy turned around to look at Dave. He slapped Dave across the face.

"Wake the fuck up, man!" shouted Tommy.

Dave looked up at Tommy, but didn't respond, a look of despair in his eyes. Roger and Graham looked behind them, the creatures in the building were getting ever closer.

"Dave, wake the fuck up, we need you!" shouted Tommy.

Dave looked into Tommy's eyes, but his face was long and pale.

"She's gone, but we're still alive, man the fuck up and be the leader we've grown to respect!" shouted Tommy.

Dave began to come around, the survival instinct was beginning to kick in, aided by the adrenaline that was now pumping through his body, his body fuelled by the impending danger. His eyes suddenly tightened and his body straightened. He had been through this before, loss on a regular and massive scale was an ordinary part of life now. He was alive, and so were at least some of his friends.

"Okay, I'm ready," said Dave.

"Let's get the fuck out of here!" shouted Tommy.

They walked quickly out of the front door. Before them was just one zombie, blocking their route to the nearest parked vehicles.

"This fucker is mine!" said Dave.

It no longer mattered that the creature had been another one of his friends, now he was utterly filled for the hatred of the zombies, choosing to ignore the faces that they wore. He ran towards the creature and thrust the head of the club hammer into its face, knocking it off its feet. Dave took the short handle in two hands and continually smashed the skull until it was nearly flat to the ground, a bloody pulp.

They looked out at the smashed gates at the entrance to their previously secure compound. One zombie was already through the gates, another only a few feet away. The zombies were sparse out in the countryside, but there were still enough to quickly overpower the survivors now that they had zombies among them in Everglade.

"Take both the Land Rovers, we cannot risk it with one!" shouted Roger.

Dave stood back upright, his hammer dripping blood at his side. He said nothing, but the entire group knew what they had to do. The vehicles each carried enough food, water and weapons to keep four people alive for a week, a precaution Roger had always insisted on, both for teams in the field, and such emergency situations as they were now in.

Dave and Roger jumped into the front of the first vehicle, whilst Tommy, Graham and Sandra took the second. The engines roared to life almost simultaneously. Dave was in the driver's seat of the Land Rover he'd spent so many months getting used to. A loud noise rang out as a zombie crashed against his door, making him jump. The vehicle was stationary whilst the engine was running, but Dave was glad of the mesh fitted over the windows.

"Time to go, Dave. This is not home for us anymore," said Roger.

"And what, we just keep driving, now just five people with nothing left in the world?" asked Dave.

"No, we do not have nothing. We have five lives, and that's worth more than solid gold bars ever were. We are the few, the lucky and capable few. We will move on, create a new home and make it better and safer than before. There are other survivors out there, we will keep living," said Roger.

Dave simply sat at the wheel, contemplating his leader's words. He knew everything that Roger said made sense, but the emotional battering that he'd received was overwhelming.

"What do you think Kailey would have wanted? For you to be morbid and lacking your characteristic cautious skills that have kept you alive, or for you to meet the same fate she did?" asked Roger.

Dave thought back to the day it had all begun. It made no sense that Kailey's death had struck him so hard, when he was quite capable of ending his best friends' lives and moving on. It had clearly amassed, finally tripping his calm persona into a depressive state. He looked over at Roger, the zombie beside him beating pointlessly at the door.

"I get it, so where to?" asked Dave.

"I'm not too sure, I suggest we get a good distance from this place, forget the horrors of this night and set up somewhere completely new with access to a whole new set of resources. Drive on, we'll hopefully find somewhere decent to stop, sleep in the trucks, and begin our new lives tomorrow," said Roger.

"You know what I wouldn't give for a kebab," said Dave.

"Where did that come from?" asked Roger.

"Just a small taste of the life I used to lead, something to look forward to, the luxuries we used to take for granted," said Dave.

"I know exactly what you mean, let's find ourselves a home, better than this one, and we'll sit down with some good ale and forget it all," said Roger.

"Sounds like a plan," said Dave.

He put his foot to the floor, spinning the wheels on the grass. The vehicle stormed towards the entrance, crushing the zombie before them. They were finally free, leaving the disaster of their greatest hope behind them, with a quarter of the people and few of the supplies.

It was a bleak day, but they at least they were alive.

CHAPTER TWELVE

RESEARCH CENTRE, HONOLULU, HAWAII

Decker and his team walked past the security desk and into the foyer of the centre. Since the outbreak the centre had been collecting as much data as it could from around the world on the creatures, their biology and anything that might help in the struggle. Walking at the front of the group, Decker approached the man sitting at the reception desk. Behind him Terry and Tony dragged the wounded prisoner with them, pushing him up against the desk.

The receptionist was startled and when he saw the bloody wounds on the man he literally stumbled backwards, very nearly falling from his chair.

"Where's Murphy? We need a word," said Decker is a serious tone.

The receptionist, now starting to regain his composure

picked up his phone, he whispered quietly into the telephone so the group of men couldn't hear him. After a short pause he replaced the handset and then looked up to Decker.

"Please sit down, Sir. Dr Murphy is sending somebody up now."

"Bullshit, we need to see him now!" shouted Decker, starting to lose his temper.

A door opened at the end of the room and two men in medical scrubs hurried towards them with a wheeled stretcher. A third man, presumably from security, followed them. He was wearing a full bio protection suit, along with additional armour and the ubiquitous Heckler & Koch MP7 on his thigh.

"What's going on?" asked Decker, as they started lifting the wounded man onto the trolley.

The security man stepped closer, putting his hand on Decker's arm. It was a mistake as Decker was not a man to be pushed around. He easily brushed the man's hand aside and twisted it around and then grabbed his elbow, locking it behind him.

"Don't fucking touch me, pal!" said an angry Decker.

Tony stepped up, flanking Decker.

"Big mistake, man. Now you're pissing him off!" he laughed.

Before the situation could escalate further an older man in a smart suit entered.

"Okay, Decker, let him go," he said in a resigned tone.

"Next time keep your dogs on a leash," said Decker as he released the man.

"Look, things have become a little more complicated than we expected. Walk with me."

Decker turned to his unit, the other five men looked tired and certainly not in the mood for a long talk on biology, infection and the usual stuff they got stuck with.

"Hey, don't worry about us, we'll see you later at the bar," said Tony with a grin.

Decker smiled, "Good work, guys, I'll see you later."

He turned back to Dr Murphy who gestured towards the door.

"Come with me, Decker. I want to show you something," he said mysteriously.

Decker went with him, they left the foyer and entered a long corridor that led to an elevator entrance. It was flanked by two men in bio-suits and body armour.

"Aren't we a little underdressed?" asked Decker.

Dr Murphy pressed a button that flashed green several times. The door hissed open and he stepped inside the glass elevator, Decker close behind. Once the doors shut he turned back to Decker.

"Good work on the capture. Those two were potentially a serious problem. Were any of your people hurt?"

"No, we went through the normal procedures when we came back. No bites, blood or wounds. I don't get it though, these guys weren't zombies."

"Well Mr Decker, you are partially correct in that respect."

The doors slid open revealing a fully equipped laboratory with at least a dozen people working at terminals. In the centre of the room was a massive screen with a three-dimensional model of a human brain rotating on it. The Doctor stopped in front of the screen and looked at it for a moment before turning back to Decker.

"As you know we've been making some progress on the virus. No, we don't have a cure but, and this is a bit but. We've managed to find a way to stabilise the virus for a time."

"How is that of any use?" asked Decker.

"A good question. First of all, tell me about your prisoner. Anything special about him?" asked the Doctor.

Decker looked a little surprised at the question before realising that of course the Doctor knew too well what was different about the man.

"Well, the two of them were both alive. They could think, reason and form an intelligent escape. When we trapped them they attempted an ambush that very nearly succeeded.

"Interesting," said Dr Murphy, "go on."

"They were stronger than they should have been, and they certainly took more damage than either you or I could in a gun fight. If I had to guess I'd say you've got a living man with some of the traits of the undead."

Dr Murphy smiled.

"Who says all security guards are simple?" he said with a chortle.

"Simple? Nice."

* * *

Jackson was already through the wire fence and was busy watching the compound, whilst the rest of his men worked their way through the narrow gap. Six months ago this would have been impossible but now, after all that had happened, the security was lax and nobody was going to bother entering areas like this one.

He double checked on the guards near the entrance. Though they weren't paying attention they would be a problem once Jackson and his men started removing the supplies. He turned around, checking that the other two were now through the fence. Jonathan was but Greg seemed to have got himself stuck. Jackson gave him a stern look and waved his hand in the direction they needed to go. With a final, almost desperate push, the man fell through the hole and into the dusty compound.

"To the generator room, let's go," said Jackson quietly. He moved off, keeping low and an ever watchful eye on the rest of the guards.

The distance was short and in seconds they were

moving along the outer wall of the nearest building. They followed it around until reaching a single room building that buzzed with the running of a series of diesel powered electrical generators.

Jackson pulled his rucksack from his back and placed it on the ground.

"Greg, watch the entrance, Jonathan, help me with these," he said.

Greg cocked his M16 rifle and moved back a few feet so he could keep the guard post in view. He lifted the rifle up to his shoulder, watching them through the magnified telescopic sight. Behind him he could hear the other two men unloading equipment. He turned quickly to see how they were doing. On the ground next to the bag were the charges, each the size of a man's fist. A sound ahead of him caught his attention and he turned back, watching the guards.

With the shaped charges out of the bag, Jackson double checked the detonators with his red beam torch before handing them to Jonathan. With a nod he crept forward, Jackson close behind. The entire building was locked down with a substantial steel door securing the entrance to the fuel, generators and transformers. Jonathan placed the first charge on the frame of the door and then placed the second on the series of reinforced pipes that fed the fuel to the generators. Jackson then passed him the detonators, a series of simple electrically triggered devices.

Though basic they were reliable, but did require them having to stay relatively close.

Both men crept back whilst Jackson unrolled the thin wire that led from him direct to the charges. Greg was still waiting as he covered the group with his rifle.

"All done?" he asked.

"Yeah, the charges are in place. Any change on the guards?" asked Jackson.

"No change, they're too busy with their game," replied Greg.

"Ok, once we take out the generators the security on most installations here will be done. We need to be the other side of the guards when everybody else turns up. Once the shooting starts we start emptying the stores," he said whilst looking at the two of them.

"What about the barracks?" asked Jonathan.

"Simple, the charges are set for thirty seconds. Once I hit the button we need to get there and be ready at the doors. When the power goes down we get inside and control the room, fast! Got it?" he asked.

The two men nodded in agreement.

"You're sure you know how to cut the power to the site?"

"Of course, all I need is the door off and I can finish the job," he said.

Jackson turned back, double checking the area. It all looked clear, just the guards on the gatehouse and the rest must still have been in the barracks. He clicked the lid open on the detonator, noting the timer set to thirty seconds, and turned the ignition key. The LED flashed three times and then switched off, indicating the unit was now active and counting down.

"Go!" he whispered to Greg whilst Jonathan took cover a short distance away.

Without looking to check on the area, he rushed out from his hiding place and moved around the building. The barracks building was adjacent to the generator room and the entrance could be fifty yards at the most. In seconds the three men were out of the danger zone and waiting on both sides of the closed door that led inside.

Jackson double-checked his watch. They had exactly twelve seconds to go before the charges went off. They were not massive charges and in fact they were specifically designed to cause the minimum of damage to the wider area. For many jobs this made them useless, but for this operation they were perfect.

Greg and Jackson both drew pistols and cocked them, making sure they were ready for the havoc that was sure to ensue. Jackson looked at him and waved his finger, indicating the charges were about to blow, Greg nodded at almost the same time as the blast. It sounded like a car backfiring and certainly much quieter than either of them expected.

Back at the generator room Jonathan was out of his

cover and running for the door. Exactly as planned the door was blasted open. He noted with satisfaction that the control and communication lines that left the building had all been destroyed by the secondary charge. Once he cut the power the only way to restore it would be for somebody else to physically come to the generator room, rather than restart it remotely. He moved inside and headed straight to the control panel. It was based around several computer terminals as well as a series of valves. He turned the valves shut, instantly causing the fuel system to stave on the generators. There would still be enough fuel to drive the system for another minute or so though.

Turning his attention to the computer terminals he pulled out the keyboard and entered the sixteen letter access password they'd been given. It was accepted and took him directly to the management screen. In the top right it indicated a communication failure with the control centre and at the bottom indicated falling fuel pressure.

"Yeah, now we're talking," said Jonathan as he started the shutdown sequence.

He double checked his work and then left the room to join the other two. Within a few seconds the sound of motors winding down started and with it the entire electrical system at the compound failed.

At the storage area Greg and Jackson waited patiently for the lights to switch off. It had been over twenty seconds now since the blast.

"Are you sure he knows what he's doing?" asked Greg.

"He'd better, we've got a schedule to keep," answered Jackson.

Jonathan rushed around the corner and into their view as the lights flickered and then died, along with the steady hum from the generator room. In his hand he held the flare gun.

Jackson nodded, giving Jonathan the signal to fire the gun. With a crack he fired directly upwards, the flare arced upwards and burst into colour, for a moment it illuminated the entire site before it started to drop back down. With the signal made Jackson then booted the door open, and ran into the storage warehouse with his pistol at the ready. Greg was close behind and Jonathan followed once he reached the door. As Greg went inside a few feet he was stopped by the surprising view of Jackson standing in the middle, his pistol hanging down at the ground.

"What is it?" asked Greg as he moved past him to look.

Jonathan entered and stepped up to the left of the small group.

"Holy shit! Did you know about this?" he asked in horror.

No fucking way!" muttered Jackson. "We've got a big problem!"

* * *

Dr Murphy and Decker examined the data on the computer screen. The images showed massive amounts of information, most of which meant little to Decker.

"I can see why you've got so many of us on retainer, with this kind of work going on," he said.

The lights in the room flickered before changing to a much lower tone of red. Some of the computer terminals switched off, though at least half stayed on. A flash from the end of the room indicated the failure of one of the emergency lights.

"What the?" said Decker as he watched the laboratory staff start running around.

Dr Murphy pressed a few keys on his terminal to bring up a map of the island. They were positioned on the outskirts of the city, though this part had been abandoned for some time.

"What's going on?" asked Decker, sounding more confused than concerned.

"Well, it's kind of obvious, but we've lost part of our power."

He moved the mouse and brought up the power system schematic for what was still working of the power grid on the islands.

"It looks like the power lines to the power station are down. What concerns me more though is that the auxiliary generators near the docks have been triggered to shut down."

"We still have power here though?" asked Decker.

"For now, but we don't have the capacity to run everything, that's why the non-critical gear has already lost power. I'm much more concerned about our storage sites that the military are supposed to be guarding."

"You're kidding? I thought they were the most secure parts of the island?"

"Well yes, that is kind of the point, Decker," answered the Doctor sarcastically.

The map of the island zoomed in close to the dock areas. A series of coloured lines indicated power and data paths to the research laboratory's various sites. The laboratory was connected to three other sites, all of them close, as well as several smaller ones on the nearest islands. The lines to the smaller islands were still displaying as solid green but three, including the docks' site, were showing as flashing red lines.

"Look here. The generators have been sabotaged. Somebody is attempting to access the sub warehouse."

"Isn't that where the…" said Decker before he was interrupted.

"Yes, we kept them there for maximum security. They're away from the population and near the sea for removal during testing."

More lights started flashing on other parts of the map.

"Damn, somebody is trying to gain access to our storage sites."

"Why, what is the point?"

"Well, being as nobody here knows what we have there, there can only be two possibilities. Number one, they want our experiments. Two they think we have something else there. Either way I need all security teams out and to the sites immediately," said Murphy.

"Could it be Ford?" asked Decker.

"Ford?" answered Dr Murphy dismissively. "I don't think so. Since he left the company he's turned to petty crime. He wasn't interested in us before the outbreak, why would he be interested now?"

"Well, he did say he would get his revenge one day, maybe this is his plan." Decker replied.

The Doctor paused for a moment, considering Decker's idea before dismissing it out of hand.

"I think that you give him more than he's due. He's an amateur. Just make sure you and your teams secure the sites and get the power back up in the next six hours."

"What if there is any contamination?" asked Decker, as he made for the door.

"We need containment. Under no circumstances can any of the experiments be allowed to get into the general population," ordered Murphy.

"Got it!" said Decker as he walked through the door. He turned and called out to the Doctor.

"Six hours, what happens then?" he asked.

Dr Murphy turned and stared hard at Decker.

"In six hours the reserve power of this facility will fail. When that happens we will lose access to all our security facilities here and at all the storage sites, including the dock warehouse."

"Fuck," muttered Decker, as he turned and left the room.

He pulled out his radio as he headed for the elevator.

"Decker here, get the team at the truck in sixty seconds, we've got a Code Red security situation. As in a holy, shit storm situation. Make sure you're packing, we are facing unknown numbers."

He entered the elevator and hit the key to take him to the surface.

"Oh, and bring the hazmat suits, all of them," he added.

"Fuck, you mean really serious," came the reply on the radio.

* * *

Jackson stood in the middle of the large storage warehouse and looked on in both awe and surprise. The area was divided up into dozens of cubicles, each like a prison cell but protected with very thick transparent plastic. The room was dimly lit by a series of low power red lights. In the centre of the room was a large pillar surrounded by half a dozen computer terminals and screens. All the computer equipment was off, apart from one small screen that showed a horizontal bar graph. Jonathan moved forward to examine the screen whilst Jackson and Greg went closer to the cells for a better look.

"According to this the life support systems are all active and running on reserve power."

"Life support?" asked Jackson to himself, as he tried to look through the thick plastic door to one of the cubicles.

"Maybe it's a hospital of some kind?" said Greg.

Jackson moved his hand along the sides of the door, trying to find a button or switch to gain access.

"I very much doubt this is a hospital. It's unmarked and is guarded by military units," said Jackson.

He put his hand in his pocket and fished out his torch. It was a small pencil type design and low power but with a very long battery life, perfectly suited to their current predicament. He pointed it at the door and hit the button. The red light gave a dim glow to the cubicle and after a few seconds Jackson could just make out the shapes inside.

"There's a bed, hey, it looks like a patient is in there," he said.

"I don't like this, don't like it one bit," said Greg from the doorway.

Jackson held his hand up to his mouth and whispered to the other two.

"Listen, they've started the diversion."

The sound of trucks' engines was coming from the direction of the main entrance and was quickly followed by gunfire, presumably from Ford and the rest of the decoy unit. A loud clatter from a heavy weapon indicated somebody was using machinegun fire.

"Greg, check on the door, we don't want any company," said Jackson whilst he continued trying to open the cubicle door.

Jonathan continued reading the data on the computer screen. The reserve power said it was on sixty seven percent, but seemed to be dropping quite fast. He read down the chart and lists of figures until he reached a small menu. At the top was a status option, it was already highlighted, presumably showing the figures further up. Below the button were two more options offering security and support. He pressed the security button and the screen immediately changed to a map of the downtown area.

"Hey, I've got something, look!" he said.

Jackson ran over, looking at the data intently. The screen showed the warehouse area off to one side and the port area and part of the downtown in the rest. Above the warehouse was a designation, it said Section 3A. At the top of the screen was a green diamond that was moving quickly down and towards the warehouse.

"What's this?" he asked.

Outside a loud noise signalled the arrival of another vehicle. Almost as soon as the sound started three holes opened up in the warehouse.

"Fuck, there's a helicopter out there. It's dropping off a security unit," shouted Greg from the doorway.

A series of bullet holes appeared along the wall.

"Fuck, get down!" shouted Jackson as he checked his Heckler & Koch MP7.

Greg dropped to the ground and started crawling over to the other two. A banging of somebody's fist on the door got their attention. It was immediately followed by a familiar voice.

"Jackson, it's Ford, are you in there?" he asked.

"Get in here!" shouted Jackson as another series of bullets struck near the entrance.

The door swung open and in ran a man in his fifties plus two men carrying carbines. Once inside the two other men pushed the door shut and moved into flanking positions. The older man smiled at Jackson as he looked around.

"Ah, I see you've found my supplies," he said.

"Supplies? I thought we were getting weapons?" asked Jackson.

"These are weapons my friend," he answered, as he moved up to the computer screen.

More gunfire came from outside.

"What about them?" asked Jackson as he pointed outside.

"We should be okay for a couple of minutes. We have two dozen men keeping them busy on the perimeter," he answered.

Ford pressed the small display and hit several options until a new screen appeared. In the centre was a restart button. Without hesitating he hit it and almost immediately half of the equipment in the warehouse switched on. First to activate was the main lighting, quickly followed by two of the computer terminals.

"The power won't last long but it's all we need," said Ford.

"I don't understand," said Greg as he watched.

"It's pretty simple," said Ford, as he walked over to the nearest cubicle.

"The company has been working on some horrific projects since the outbreak, some of them before then. I've suspected for some time they were doing this though."

"Doing what?" asked Greg.

The lights in the cubicle lit up showing the bed and the subject lying down. It was either dead or unconscious, or perhaps sleeping.

"Each of these people is infected from the original outbreak in Alaska. The company has been working on them for nearly a year now, trying to find ways to use the infection."

"Why do they want to use the infection, why not cure it?"

"Cure?" said Ford with a smile. "There is no cure. They can increase the time it takes to kill the host, increase the virulence, in some circumstances even give the infected person the ability to demonstrate some of the traits of the undead before finally succumbing to death and the normal zombification."

"So what are we doing here?" asked Jonathan.

"That's the right question," said Ford, as he pressed a final button.

One of the guards stepped forward and handed him a dark object. The guard then pulled a mask out and placed it on his face. Ford opened his bag and did the same before turning to Jackson.

"What's going on?" he asked suspiciously.

A bright flash came from the roof that forced the men to the ground in pain. It was followed by at least half a dozen shadows dropping from the ceiling to the ground.

Jackson rolled over, realising that this was probably a stun grenade of some kind. His MP7 was lying on the ground, just out of his reach. He pushed out as far as he could go but it wasn't enough. A heavy boot kicked the weapon out of the way before rough hands lifted him up.

Jackson was surprised to see the men were two of Ford's guards.

"What the fuck?" he shouted, his head still spinning.

Jonathan and Greg were up against the wall with their hands in the air. He turned his head, watching the group of armed men working their way around the warehouse. Jackson noticed them pressing an unmarked pad on each cubicle that revealed a keypad. A short flurry of presses opened the doors, revealing the patients that lay sleeping on their beds.

"Take them to the trucks," ordered Ford.

"Ford, what are you doing?" shouted Jackson.

Ford continued moving through the building, ignoring the pleas from Jackson as he was taken from the warehouse. The sound of the battle had ceased outside to be replaced by the men shouting. As his eyes adjusted to the darkness he spotted over a dozen dead soldiers in the compound and one truck was burning near the gate.

"They didn't have to die!" shouted Jackson, as he and his two men were dragged to one of the waiting pickup trucks.

The three were thrown into the back and watched by four men, all wearing balaclavas and each armed with automatic weapons. Jonathan tried to get away and was hit with a rifle butt to the back of the head.

"Keep your head down, this won't take long," he said.

"Why are you doing this?" pleased Greg.

"Shut the fuck up. We've got our own plans for you, and them!" he said, as he pointed to the warehouse.

From the doorway the first of the wheeled trolleys was pushed out and towards the trucks. More trolleys appeared as the patients were removed from the facility. Another group of men in black tactical clothing were busy placing a series of what looked like demolition charges on the buildings.

"You're gonna blow the place!" said Greg angrily.

"Why tie us up?" he added.

"Who do you think is gonna get the blame?" he said with a laugh.

CHAPTER THIRTEEN

NEW SOUTH WALES, AUSTRALIA

The chiefs had been sitting around for an hour now trying to think of a way to sort out the situation. Some of them wanted to drive in and attempt a roof rescue across hatches. Others thought this would lead to more vehicles being trapped.

"Give me the Beast, I'll manage it," said Jake.

The Beast was what they all lovingly referred to as the Land Train truck. The chiefs looked at Jake thoughtfully. Jake was a man the entire group trusted, he was a tough old boot, capable and reliable.

"You want to risk the only vehicle we have to tow the fuel?" asked Chris.

"I know it isn't ideal, but it has enough torque to tear down a building, it's the only one which has what it takes to get the job done," said Jake.

The men sat around the table rubbed their chins and thought, but nobody spoke.

"Look, this is the only realistic and useful solution that has been presented. Unless there's a majority objection, I'm going ahead, so either speak now or hold your tongues," said Jake.

The chiefs still sat silent, not wanting to commit to a dangerous plan, but none wanting to condemn their friends either.

"Right, Wilson, get the trailers unhooked from the Beast, we leave in ten," said Jake.

Ten minutes later Jake was strapping on his equipment beside the Beast. His granddaughter Amy was beside him. Still a teenager, she had shown herself to be as useful as her grandfather, being accurate with a rifle and cool headed. The trailers were now disconnected and Wilson walked around to join Jake.

"You don't have to come, we can handle this," said Jake.

"No way you're taking my baby from me. Only one who drives this rig is me," said Wilson.

Jake smiled, full well appreciating the man's support.

"Right, mount up, let's get going."

They leapt into the big rig and Wilson fired up the 16.4 litre, 610hp diesel engine. The rumble of the engine was a reassuring sound to all aboard, knowing that no mass of zombies in the world would be able to stop them.

"So what's the plan?" asked Wilson.

"Smash our way in, take the crew across the roofs, and then bug out," said Jake.

"What about Road Hog?" asked Wilson.

"Nothing we can do about that, but it's just a vehicle, we can find another, people are the priority," said Jake.

"Okidoki," said Wilson.

The rig driver pulled a chrome .44 revolver from the dashboard, opened the cylinder to check it was fully loaded, and then threw the cylinder shut and put it on the dash near the steering wheel. As the vehicle pulled away, the occupants could see the remaining survivors watching them drive off. The faces of those left behind were nothing but worry and sadness.

Back at the Hog, the crew of five was sitting at the dining table, eating chocolate and swilling cans of Solo Strong. They sat in a disturbingly calm state, all knowing they could do nothing but wait.

"Card game anyone?" asked Connor.

"Go for it," said Bruce.

Connor got the deck out from a side drawer. It was heavily used, a common pastime when on the road for this crew. Bruce, being the leader of the group, was the most concerned as all the others would assume nothing less than a full rescue attempt by the group, but with him missing who knows what could happen.

"You know what we need, a helicopter," said Connor.

"No shit, that's really helpful," said Dylan.

"Alright, alright! At least he's staying positive!" said Bruce.

"And what if no one comes for us?" asked Dylan.

"Then we'll improvise and overcome, we aren't going to die here," said Bruce.

"Nice to see someone is confident," said Dylan.

"Yeah, what is the point in anything else? Be positive and we have a chance, be a miserable sad bastard and you may just die here," said Bruce.

Dylan went silent, humiliated into shutting up. The more he thought about Bruce's words, the more he actually agreed, perhaps they would get out. All around them was the ever droning sound of the zombie groans. Their vehicle swaying ever so slightly with the mass of creatures continually pushing and pulling at anything they could reach.

The cards were being handed out around the table when they heard a wrenching sound and then something break beside them. They quickly looked over, just in time to see glass shatter before them onto the carpet of the RV. The creatures had managed to break some of the mesh from a side window and had smashed the window. Hands reached up for the window frame and a creature was already pulling itself up and into the vehicle. Bruce drew his .45 and fired immediately, the beast tumbled back onto the horde below.

"Find something to seal the hole!" shouted Bruce.

Dylan drew his shotgun and Connor his hand crossbow, whilst the other two ran to the back of the vehicle to find something. The window was fairly high on the side of the vehicle, which was at least fortunate, meaning the creatures were bottlenecked. Connor fired his weapon, the bolt slightly deflecting off the next creature's inner nose bone and sliding into the eye socket. Blood dripped from the eye ball and socket as the body slumped back down.

"Gordon, get a fucking shift on!" shouted Bruce.

The three men fired, more frantically now, as the horde began to gain a stronger hold on their breach in the vehicle's wall. Gordon was looking around everywhere, finally he grabbed hold of the door to Bruce's bedroom, he pulled it hard, but the strong hinges were too much for him. Drake drew is hammer from his belt and smashed the hinges away from the wood they were attached to. Shots rang out behind him as once again Bruce's pistol was empty.

The two men ran back to the breach of the RV to see Dylan fire both barrels in quick succession, clearing the way.

"Out the way!" shouted Gordon.

The defenders moved back as the two with the door ran into place and shoved it into position. Before they could get it flush with the window frame a zombie got its fingers through. Bruce immediately drew his machete and cut down against them, severing three. The door went flush against the frame and the two men put their bodyweight against it to keep it in place.

"Get anything you can to wedge this in and strengthen it!" said Bruce.

Following Gordon's example Connor smashed the door off the toilet and shower room, and ran back to place it in front of the current blockage for extra strength. Bruce ripped the table from the seating area and wedged it between the doors at the seats opposite, it held them in place. The rest of the men began piling things around the barricade.

"Right, that should hold for at least a while, but I bloody hope we get some help soon," said Bruce.

They looked back at where they'd had been sitting, their playing cards scattered across the floor, most of the cushions taken and used in the barricade. This was a dire situation, their vehicle's defences were compromised and they had nowhere left to play. Bruce sat down on the floor against a sidewall.

"Make sure all your weapons are loaded and in order, and you're ready to go at a second's notice. Either someone comes to our rescue, or we have to fight our way out of here on foot," said Bruce.

"That's suicide!" said Dylan.

"No, suicide is staying in here once our last defence is finally breeched, I'd rather have a chance getting through that crowd than to be trapped in here. Anyway, it's a last resort," said Bruce.

The other men relaxed, resting against cupboards or sitting down. Each of them checked their weapons and ammunition and got everything ready. The horde outside continually tested their defences, trying to break anything they could. All of the crew knew that they probably had an hour left of safety at the most. Over the groans of the creatures outside, Bruce suddenly noticed the sound of something rather more industrial.

"Listen, can you hear that?" shouted Bruce.

"What?" asked Connor.

"Just listen, sounds like a vehicle," said Bruce.

They all stood and listened intently, the noise was getting louder and louder. Bruce went to the back of the vehicle and peered out of the barred window in his bedroom. The creatures at the back of the crowd were already beginning to turn around and pay attention. This could only be a good thing.

"Alright boys, this could be our way out. Make sure you're ready, get the ladder in position, we'll be going out the roof," said Bruce.

He looked back to see the Beast storm into view five hundred yards ahead, the sheer size and power of the thing overcame him with joy.

"It's the Beast!" Bruce shouted.

They all cheered, delighted at the fact that their fellow

survivors had not forgotten them. The huge Road Train truck hit the first few zombies, it passed through them as if they were paper, their bodies crumpling and being thrown aside. The Beast had the characteristic huge chrome bars across the front, taller than a man, though dulled and dirty now from a year of travel.

A hundred yards later the monstrous truck hit the dense horde, the initial twenty zombies were crushed against the ones in front of them. The huge roo bars of the vehicle ploughed a channel through the bloody mess, as Moses parted the sea. No doubt the stricken crew of the Hog saw this monster as their saviour in such a hopeless situation.

Bruce was astonished about the nerve and initiative shown by his fellow survivors. He'd become the leader of the group quite naturally, by showing the most leadership. It always concerned him then when the responsibility fell on someone else's shoulders. Bruce had always had to trust other people to work alongside him, but trusting others to be in charge when his life was at stake was a totally different matter.

The Beast was smashing its way ever closer to the Hog, but the weight and mass of the horde being crushed against them forced the RV flat against the shop and was beginning to buckle parts of the vehicle. Finally, the truck drew to a stop in parallel with the Hog and just a few feet away. The horde immediately re-established their position around the two vehicles, flooding them. The high sides were too much for the zombies to overcome, but some were already attempting to climb onto the footsteps and bonnet of the Beast.

"Get up on the roof, now!" shouted Bruce.

Dylan got up on the ladder and swung the roof hatch open and he climbed out onto the flat top. He looked across to see the hatch of the Beast opening on top of the caravan body that had been retrofitted to the frame. Jake clambered out onto the roof, followed by Amy. Jake pulled out a ladder from the hatch and swung it across onto the roof of the Hog forming a causeway.

Bruce was the last one up onto the roof of the Hog, Dylan and Connor were up on top, whilst the other two were already safely across and jumping down the hatch. Amy racked the lever of her Winchester and fired at a zombie trying to clamber from the bonnet onto the roof. It collapsed onto its back on the bonnet.

"Come on!" shouted Jake.

"Connor, get your arse over there!" shouted Bruce.

Connor made his way slowly across the ladder, whilst Bruce spotted a zombie beating on the driver's door of the Beast. He drew his colt and took careful aim with both hands, firing at the back of the knee. The shot caused the creature's leg to fail and its body tumbled back into the crowd.

"Dylan, go!" shouted Bruce.

Amy continued to fire carefully aimed shots at the zombies attempting to clamber up from the front of the vehicle. Bruce holstered his pistol and got onto the ladder, he ran across it, not wanting to stop or lose balance. He stumbled clumsily over onto the roof of the Beast, Jake taking his arm to help him the last part.

"You're a life saver!" shouted Bruce.

"Yet again, now get your arse inside!" shouted Jake.

Dylan was making his way down the roof hatch as Jake picked up the ladder and passed it on down with him.

"Amy, honey, time to go!" shouted Jake.

The girl had a zombie in sight that had got up onto the bonnet and was climbing onto the roof, she pulled the trigger, but only heard a click, the rifle was empty. She quickly moved back to the hatch, Jake helping her in. Bruce raised his pistol and fired a shot into the skull of the beast, killing it instantly. Jake was clambering down the hatch.

"Bruce, let's go!" shouted Jake.

Bruce moved to the hatch but looked up one last time at the Hog, which had been his home for almost a year. It was a sad day, to have had to leave everything behind once again. Looking to the front of the vehicle, more creatures were already making their way up towards the roof.

"Bruce, come on!" shouted Dylan.

He put his legs in through the hatch and dropped in, pulling the hatch over behind him and clamping it down.

"Let's get this thing moving!" shouted Bruce.

"Wilson! Get going!" shouted Jake.

The throaty engine roared as Wilson put some power down, the powerhouse of a vehicle lurched forward, feeling like it was pulling a heavy load due to the mass before it, but nothing would stop it moving. The huge chrome bars pushed their way through the massive horde for a few minutes until they were finally free. Wilson got a few hundred yards up the road when he swung wide, and stopped, turning the monster around, now facing the horde once more.

"What are you doing?" asked Jake.

"That ain't the way we want to be going. This is, and I'll be damned if those bastards will stop me!" shouted Wilson.

Wilson again put the power down, this time with nothing to stop him gaining speed. The truck roared back towards the horde, reaching a good steady speed.

"Fuck you all!" screamed Wilson.

They hit the crowd, the occupants feeling a jolt as the speed was reduced but not stopped. Blood spewed up across the windscreen and bodies crumpled and were knocked aside. They were again trawling through the massive horde. Moments later they broke free, and Bruce looked out the back window to see the result of their work. The killing streak of the Beast was barely noticeable now as the horde simply merged again, shambling towards them as they drove off into the distance. Bruce looked back at Jake, grabbed his hand and shook it.

"You're a true gent," said Bruce.

"No worries, mate," said Jake.

"That goes for your girl and that crazy bitch up front too," said Bruce.

The crew lay back on the seating that was available, truly relieved.

"How many did we lose?" asked Bruce.

"Just Walter," said Jake.

"We all knew he'd screw up at some point, and it only cost him his own life," said Bruce.

"Yes, but that was still one too many."

"True," said Bruce.

It felt like an age to get back to the rest of the convoy. All of the men were still wearing their full equipment and were sitting in the hot trailer, the open windows providing very little fresh air. Finally they reached the encampment where all of the survivors were gathered to greet then, having seen the huge truck coming from miles away.

The vehicle came to a halt thirty yards from the nearest RV. Bruce staggered out, hot, tired and bothered. He was glad to be alive, but feeling rather disillusioned by the state of the group.

"What the hell happened out there?" asked Keith.

"We got greedy, we got careless, and it cost us one man's life, a vehicle and a shit load of supplies," said Bruce.

"Would you care to explain it to us?" asked Keith.

Bruce walked up to Keith furiously. He grabbed him by his shirt.

"No, I fucking wouldn't you muppet! You can sit on your arse and complain all you like, but the reality is shit happens, sometimes it can be avoided, and this is a case of it. The group has become lax lately, too much drink, too little focus," said Bruce.

Bruce shoved Keith away who stayed silent. The group that had come to greet them was expecting to celebrate their success, but Bruce had lowered the tone. He was furious with the lax state that had overcome them all, and angry with himself for being in part a cause of it as much as anyone else. Bruce paced up and down, them all waiting for him to speak.

"You want to celebrate, don't you? Celebrate what? This is total shit, and the only people who should feel happy with their actions today are the three who came to get us, the only people who acted in good conscience with a sensible and safe course of action."

The crowd was gripped by Bruce's words, shocked by his negative outlook and sudden serious turn, but entirely focused.

"We need to have a serious think about our future, because we cannot continue this way. The cities are too dangerous and the safer supplies are running thinner. This lifestyle will keep us going for maybe another year, but the food and fuel isn't going to last forever," said Bruce.

"What do you suggest?" asked Keith.

"I don't have a suggestion. All I'm saying is we must all give some serious consideration to the way we act each and every day, and how we intend to stay alive for the years to come," said Bruce.

"But what do we do now?" asked Keith.

"Now, we have what we have, and there's a city right next to us full of undead fuckers. We need to get as far from it as possible. Saddle up, we're moving out right now, I want a new vehicle before the week is over, and we're heading on to new lands," said Bruce.

CHAPTER FOURTEEN

MID-WEST, UNITED STATES

Madison awoke a half hour after sunrise, earlier than she had in a long time, the impeding threat being enough to keep her from her usual deep sleep. Still wearing the clothes from the day before, she slipped her shoes on and walked out of the house to see what was going on. Half of the town's people were already up and out of their houses, beginning the preparations for the day ahead. Jack was gassing his truck up with jerry cans, outside the church where he'd left if the day before. Wells walked out of the church with a loudhailer in hand. He held it up to his lips.

"Everyone not on guard is to meet in the square in fifteen minutes," he said.

Dale and his brother rode into view, each of their horses tugging a truck along slowly into the centre of the town.

"You're stars!" shouted Madison.

"You just better hope they come back in the condition they started in!"

"You mean dirty, dented and out of gas?" asked Jack.

They chuckled. Both loved their trucks but were glad to finally see them being put to work again. The brothers unhooked the horses from their vehicles and walked over to the fuel bowser that was parked up across the street from the church. They began filling Jerry cans that were stacked alongside it to get their vehicles ready for their new drivers. The people were already amassing in the square, much quicker than Wells had ordered, which pleased him. The Pastor again got up onto the bed of Jack's truck, looking up to see the last few people arrive and waiting for him to speak.

"Firstly I want to thank you all for your prompt arrival, the safety of our homes is at stake, and the responsibility to defend it falls equally among us all!" said Wells.

The crowd listened intently, still silent and unsure of exactly what the next few days were going to involve. Most of the crowd was well armed with rifles, shotguns and handguns, as well as an assortment of close quarter weapons. There wasn't a person among them that was completely unarmed, just as per their rules. Pastor Wells was wearing a black combat vest over his usual clothing, the white collar still visible, a thigh leg holster slung on his right hip with a glistening revolver hanging from it.

This sight was a shock to them as he'd always carried his handgun concealed, but now saw the necessity to be equal among his people.

"The next few days are going to be some of the hardest, if not the worst days we have ever seen, but they have one saving grace. When this war began we were caught unawares, with our trousers down some might say. Survivors were scattered, with few supplies and no hope of a home or community. That is not the fight we face now, now the ball is in our court. We're working as one, as an organised and determined community. We have the supplies, the manpower, the ammunition and the skills we need. We're going to fight these creatures, and we are going to send them back to hell!" shouted Wells.

The crowd cheered, inspired by their spiritual leader to do the very best they could. Many of the people waved guns in the air, an unnerving sight after a pastor's speech, but a comforting one nonetheless.

"Greg, you're in charge of construction, get us some sturdy walls around the church and surrounding buildings, be sure to leave us as escape route to the east, God forbid we should need it. Madison, you're on vehicle duty, assemble as many vehicles you can, a selection of buses and trucks, get them operational and armoured up. I will now leave you with Jack, who will handle the combat side of things, good luck and God speed," said Wells.

"We move out in ten minutes, be sure you have plenty

of ammunition on all the trucks, and that the Molotov's are safely secured. Also be sure to have water and basic food onboard. All who are coming with me assemble here once the trucks are ready so I can explain the strategy. That's it, good luck to all of you," said Jack.

The town square erupted into motion, each person going about their appointed job. Ten minutes later the drivers and crews of the vehicles, thirty five in total, were assembled at the vehicles, all awaiting Jack's final words.

"It'll be about a four hour drive to get out to the horde, so conserve food and water. We have a lot of ammunition, but there's also a shit load of zombies. We'll have a simple policy. We stop three hundred yards in front of the horde and turn around so we face back towards home. We'll stay in a line, three vehicles wide on the road, with a truck each side on the grass. Nobody begins firing until they reach a hundred yards and then keep firing till they reach thirty yards, no less than twenty. We then fire up the trucks and drive on a hundred yards, repeating the process. No truck moves without the group, and no one fires until I give the word each time we stop. Drivers will be our eyes to the sides and rear, all clear?" said Jack.

"How about the Molotovs?" asked Billy.

"They have a pretty short range so they'll be the last things we use each time the horde closes to twenty yards. I want engines running every time the horde reaches fifty yards. If at any time a truck won't start or move, you jump to another and leave it behind. Remember, headshots are what bring these bastards down best, so use your ammunition wisely, anything else?" said Jack.

The crowd shook their heads, there was probably a lot more Jack should tell them, but time was a luxury they didn't have.

"A couple more things, those with shotguns, use the buckshot and solid slugs we have as much as possible, save the birdshot for the defence of Babylon where the ranges will better suit it. Also, once the firing begins, we don't want to be doubling up targets, we'll be in a line of five vehicles, therefore divide the horde up into five quadrants, in proportion to where your vehicle is in our formation, and keep your shooting to those areas. Right, let's load up!" shouted Jack.

The fighters poured into the vehicles as the engines fired up. Madison and Wells watched them from the entrance of the church as they drove out of the town. Madison had her beloved AK slung on her shoulder as ever, though she knew it would likely not fire a shot for a few days.

"It's time we all got on," said Wells.

"Alright guys, let's move!" shouted Madison.

The four men assigned to her followed her down the southern road, towards her old school where she hoped to find some working buses. The men she led had little respect for her before the Zompoc, but the fact she was the Pastor's daughter forced them to at least be publicly polite. However, her capable skills over the last year had made them all re-consider their opinions of Madison, and they were now happy to work alongside her. One of the men pulled a horse with four Jerry cans slung over its back, two gas and two diesel. Another man pulled a donkey along with all manner of tools slung over it, from crowbars to sledge hammers.

"We'll go for the buses to begin with, they'll allow us to haul the maximum number of people and supplies, so they are our priority," said Madison.

It was an hour's walk to her old school, it being the other side of town, a walk she had become so familiar with, but it now shared little with her memories. Despite the survivors' efforts to maintain the area they now called Babylon, the edge of town had been left to decay. Many of the shop windows were smashed from either fighting or the gathering of supplies. Old clothing and paperwork was scattered across the street, with dirt and dust everywhere. It looked like it was a ghost town.

The group finally reached the school, almost all of the old metal railings and wire fence having been taken by the survivors to fortify their homes and vehicles. The dusty old yellow bus was already in view, with the rear of another behind it. They carefully ventured towards the vehicles, weapons drawn. This part of town was abandoned, but there was always the threat of zombies in any area that wasn't protected at all times. Madison led the way past the first vehicle, the second's front end was parked inside a large workshop. The hood was off the bus and parts and tools were strewn about, clearly it was being worked on a year before.

"How bad is it?" asked Madison.

Joey stepped a little closer, a young and capable mechanic. He stuffed his head into the engine bay and tinkered around for a minute before looking up.

"I don't know exactly what's wrong here, but I guess it was a big job, it'll likely need a day to fix, assuming we can find all the parts," said Joey.

"That won't do, leave it, let's check the other, the keys should be in that office in the corner," said Madison.

Joey grabbed the keys and boarded the bus, turning the ignition the fuel gauge was on empty, having already been siphoned. The big diesel block turned over and kicked into life, black smoke bellowing from its exhaust.

"Cut it, and get some fuel in that tank!" shouted Madison.

"Fucking hell, always wanted to drive one of these things," said Joey.

"Let's work on getting this bus up and running today, so we know we at least have one solid vehicle to haul people and kit. Joey, I want you to give it a good look over underneath, make sure everything is solid. The rest of you, time to go looking for any bars, mesh, anything you can get. I want this bus fully operational and armoured before the day is out. I also want some kind of plough on the front, we may have to force our way through those bastards, and this could well be the vehicle to do it. I'll stay here on watch whilst Joey's working," said Madison.

* * *

Far from the long boring drives Jack was used to, it was an anxious drive to face their enemy, as it always was when you were en route to a battle. Jack had been praying to find nothing, to discover that they'd changed direction, or were just a figment of his imagination, or that the numbers weren't as large as he had estimated. Finally after several hours the horde came into view, that same sea of foulness that had shocked them the first time. He could hear the people sitting in the truck bed gasp at the sight of them. Jack rolled down his window and slid the divider across behind him.

"This is it lads, follow my lead and stick to the plan!" shouted Jack.

They drove up in front of the horde, a column along the road and track beside it for as long as they could see. The vehicles turned around in convoy like a snake, until they were facing back towards Babylon. Jack's lead truck came to a slow halt and the other vehicles forked off around him, forming up in line. He stepped out from the passenger seat, his bushmaster carbine slung across his body. Jack was now wearing a combat vest over a t-shirt, holstered pistol and sunglasses, looking like a private contractor from the human war he'd once fought in.

"This is it people, you have a few minutes before they get within range, be sure that all your weapons are in order and ammunition within reach, have the Molotovs ready too!" called Jack.

The horde shambled on, completely unaffected by the hunting party's presence. Slides racked and bolts clicked as the survivors made themselves ready for the first wave. Jack swung his grab bag around to the side of his body and threw the lid open, ready to dispose of his empty magazines, he was stood beside the bed of his truck. All went silent among the hunting pack, all ready, only awaiting their command to release hell upon the creatures. Sweat dripped from their brows as the heat beat down on them and the stress weighed heavy.

"Fire!" shouted Jack.

The first shots rang out like a musket volley, followed by a random but almost continuous sound of gun shots, as the different weapons and users fired at their own speed. Bodies dropped across the frontline of the horde, the column behind them simply stepping through or over their dead and crippled. The guns kept firing, blood splattered and bodies fell along the line, but the horde kept going. Finally they were within forty yards and getting nearer.

"Molotovs! Get the Molotovs!" shouted Jack.

The crews each began to take up the first of their Molotovs, lighting the rags that hung from them.

"Cease fire! Now!" shouted Jack.

Five Molotovs were hurled against the crowd. Two struck the very nearest, shattering and sending flames across the front of their column. The other three disappeared into a fiery mass among them. Those creatures behind the ones on fire began to slow as their path was blocked, with others forcing through in a more dispersed manner.

"That's it, let's move!" ordered Jack.

He jumped onto the edge of the truck bed as the vehicles lurched forward and ambled along the track. All of the crew began to put their weapons down to cool and take up their second weapons. Jack unclipped his carbine and sat it in the truck bed, picking up his rifle of the same calibre which shared magazines. He banged on the top of the roof, signifying the line to stop, before leaping off the side.

"Right, that was a good first run. Keep calm, keep the routine and we'll be home for dinner before you know it!" Jack shouted to them.

This mass culling continued all day, and the column rolled into Babylon at nine o'clock that evening. The westerly wall was now complete, a combination of overturned trucks, trailers, cars and building supplies, all lashed together. The five vehicles came to a halt outside the church as before. The crews were dusty and exhausted, many slept through the journey home. Wells stepped out of his church to greet them, alongside Madison.

"Jack, how did it go?" asked Wells.

"We gave them hell, but I have no idea if it will be enough, maybe we'll have a better idea after tomorrow," said Jack.

"Maybe tomorrow! This is our home we're talking about, everything we have fought and died over!" shouted Wells.

Jack looked up with a disgusted look at the Pastor. He stormed up to the man and grabbed him by the straps of his combat vest.

"How about you show a little appreciation?"

"I, I," said Wells.

"We're all working our god damn asses off, doing the best we can with what we have. If that isn't enough, then that's simply it!" shouted Jack.

"Alright, I'm sorry, I just need this to work," said Wells.

"We all do," said Jack.

"Let's call it a day and sit down for some food, guys," said Madison.

"Sure, let's do that," said Wells.

"Listen up! Time for chow, but once you're done, make sure before you turn in you thoroughly clean and oil all the weapons you used. We need them in full working order for the morning," said Jack.

The next two days continued in much the same fashion as the first, passing much quicker than anyone could have imagined. Finally on the fourth day, the tired survivors awoke for what they knew would be their last chance. The horde was now just ten miles from Babylon when the survivors woke up for that final chance.

Madison stepped out of her house to see Jack's teams loading their weapons beside the trucks, the rest of the populace assembling weapons alongside the makeshift walls to their town. She climbed a car that was forming a firing step behind an overturned tractor trailer. She gasped at the sight of the horde in the distance, like a dark snake creeping towards them. Madison climbed back down and walked towards to the church.

"I don't care how many there are, you get out there and fight!" shouted Wells.

"We're just wasting ammunition, we can't stop them!" shouted Jack.

"Then we will fight them on the walls!" said Wells.

"Do you know anything about sieges?" asked Jack.

"Stop it! Now!" shouted Madison.

The two men looked at her, already calmed slightly by her presence.

"Jack wants us to just pack up and leave our homes," said Wells.

"And what if we don't do that?" asked Madison.

"Then the town will be swamped, we'll be trapped here,

assuming the defences hold. We'd just have to hope to kill them over time, but that is not likely," said Jack.

"What other options do we have?" she asked.

"They could go out and fight as they have the last few days, and hope to whittle their numbers down enough to make the defence possible," said Wells.

"Jack, maybe leaving is the best thing to do, but what about morale. After all this work, we just leave? That's it? So what if we can't beat the horde, wouldn't everyone feel a whole lot better that we had at least given it our best shot?" asked Madison.

Jack sighed. He was annoyed about having to give civilian emotions a consideration when in a military situation, but the harsh reality that almost everyone he commanded was a civilian struck the message home to him.

"Yeah, I guess they might," said Jack.

"That's the spirit!" Wells said.

"Madison, get all the food, water, fuel and ammunition onto your vehicles as you can, everything my people aren't using. Get Greg's group to help, they have nothing left to do. We'll head out and fight them, give them hell. But make sure those vehicles are ready to roll east. I promise I'll fight them, but I give no promise that we can win," said Jack.

"Thank you, Jack," said Wells.

"Alright people, mount up!" shouted Jack.

The vehicles rolled out to cheers from those left in the town, a small but enthusiastic crowd.

"Right everyone, I want all the supplies we can get, food, water, ammunition, clothing and bedding too. We have three buses and three trucks. Load all of the supplies onto the pickups, bedding into the buses. Those vehicles may become our homes for some time, so let's be sure they're as comfortable as they can be!" said Madison.

Two hours later the convoy was as prepared as it could be, with enough supplies as they could take and still have space for people. The twenty people that were left in Babylon took to the walls with their weapons, both in preparation to fight, and to rest from their rushed labour. Wells sat down on top of an overturned bus alongside his daughter. He took out the chromed .44 Smith and Wesson from his thigh holster and popped open the chamber, to be certain it was fully loaded. He clicked the cylinder back into place and rested the gun in his lap, still in hand.

* * *

An hour later the trucks were reaching the walls of Babylon. They'd killed hundreds, perhaps thousands, but the bodies were not in sight, the massive horde covering their dead.

"You know we can't win here," said Madison.

"Yes, I know. But it was a dream that I had to at least hold onto for as long as I could," said Wells.

"Where will we go now?" asked Madison.

"Wherever God leads us," he replied.

"Then to some place warm and safe I hope," whispered Madison.

The Pastor smiled, before standing up and looking out across the few worried defenders that stood on the walls around them, watching the endless horde of evil.

"This is it, we did our best, we had a good life here, and we will create one as good or better somewhere else. Greg, I want you on the easterly gate to allow the trucks in. Once they're through, we'll have just five minutes to gather what last supplies we have and then leave. I want everyone else on the walls with me!" shouted Wells.

The guns below them rang out for the final time. The horde was just a hundred yards from the improvised walls now.

"Fire when ready!" shouted Wells.

Madison knelt down and shouldered her AK, she had for months wanted the opportunity to use it, though this now left a sour taste in her mouth. She flicked the selector switch onto semi-automatic, and opened fire. Shots rang out across the walls in a haphazard fashion, barely making any difference to the horde's advance. Jack's trucks arrived in the square just as the zombies hit the walls.

"Everyone out! Grab everything useful you can, then

onto the buses!" shouted Jack.

Madison felt the vehicle beneath her buckle, as the sheer pressure of the horde forcing against it was already putting a huge strain on the defences they'd taken days to build.

"These walls aren't going to hold much longer!" shouted Madison.

"I know, there's nothing more we can do here, get to the buses!" shouted Wells.

Every survivor left immediately, leaping down from their positions and heading for the vehicles, none wanting to risk being left alone to the mercy of the beasts.

"Jack, that wall is gonna go any minute, we have to leave now!"

Before Jack could answer Wells a section of the wall broke in two, where a bus and trailer were connected, the horde forced a gap and the zombies were pouring through.

"Greg, get the gate open! Everyone else, to the vehicles!" shouted Jack.

Madison, Wells and Jack lifted their weapons and fired everything they had into the oncoming creatures, before jumping into the truck bed of Jack's Dodge.

"Let's go!" shouted Jack.

The vehicle's wheels spun as it lurched forward, storming towards the gate. They could already see the re-enforced doors being slammed shut on the buses as they raced past them, the other trucks following suit. Madison looked back to see the vehicles each in turn passing out through the gate after them.

"That's it, that's all of them, we made it!" cried Madison.

"Yeah, we did, for today," said Wells.

"Where to, boss?" asked Jack.

"I was the natural leader with a community that used its church as a centre. But we have again embarked on a new life, one where you are that leader. Will you step up to the task?" said Wells.

"I'll do my best," said Jack.

"That's all God ever asks of anyone," said Wells.

"Oorah!" shouted Jack.

CHAPTER FIFTEEN

HONOLULU, HAWAII

Decker examined his maps as the Mercedes Unimog made its way along the debris filled road. Since the outbreak many of these parts of the city had been abandoned and without maintenance and clearing operations many of the roads were blocked and filled with vegetation, waste and other junk that impeded their progress. The radio crackled.

"Sir, we're in position. We can see the warehouse burning, we can't see any people on the ground," came the voice.

"Any sign of vehicles? They must have got there somehow," asked Decker.

"Negative, we can hear gunfire though. Do you want us to move in?"

"Stay where you are. We need eyes on the warehouse, keep in contact."

"Wait, I've got movement one block away. There's a column of vehicles in the street, but they aren't moving. Hey, I can.." the radio whistled and then cut out.

"Fuck!" shouted Decker as he tried to regain contact. It was no good though, either their gear was down or they had been eliminated.

He turned to his unit, each of the men was sitting on the uncomfortable bench seating. The Unimog was a cross between an agricultural off-road vehicle and a military truck. It was tall, heavy and unstoppable but lacked all the niceties of a civilian vehicle.

"We've got a problem," said Decker.

"No shit," answered Terry with a grin.

Decker lay the map out in front of him so the others could see.

"What we know is that all contact has been lost with the 3A facility. The guard unit is not responding. We have no data or power connections and our recon element providing overwatch reports the facility is burning and a column of vehicles is nearby."

"Sounds like a major operation. They must have come in by vehicle as no aircraft were detected right?" asked Tony.

"Exactly. We have a chance to catch them if we're quick. The main route from the facility passes under this rail bridge here before hitting the intersection and four different routes. If we hurry we could establish an ambush there before they can escape and finish whatever it is they're doing."

"Yeah, I like it. How long since we lost contact?" asked Terry.

"Twelve minutes but there's another problem. They may have taken out our recon unit, if that's the case then they may have more people out there than we thought. If we're fast we have a good chance of cutting them off," answered Decker, "any questions?"

He looked around the group. Tony raised his hand.

"Yeah, what are they doing? Why are they hitting the compound?" he asked.

"Good point. Right now we don't know. My guess is either they want to cause damage, but more likely they want to take samples."

"Samples?" asked Terry.

"Yeah, this is an offsite medical facility for the company. Our orders are to contain or destroy. Under no circumstances can anything get out of the area," he added.

"Understood?" he asked.

The rest of the unit nodded in agreement.

"Okay then, make sure your gear is ready. We'll be there in four minutes."

He climbed forward so he could speak to the driver in the crew section whilst the rest of the group double-checked their weapons for the impending confrontation.

* * *

Jackson, Greg and Jonathan were still tied up securely in the back of the truck when they spotted the first zombie. Jackson thought it was one of the soldiers at first before he realised it had stumbled out of the warehouse. He nudged Greg.

"Looks like they missed one."

"Hey, didn't we see that guy inside before they kicked us out?"

Jackson nodded and then twisted his head to the right, trying to point out something else.

"Can you see that? Look!"

Greg strained to see where he was looking. On the side of the warehouse was a storage bunker about the size of a small truck and from it a cloud of vapour was leaking out. Near the ground were the bodies of four of the soldiers who had been detailed to protect the site. The vapour must have been heavier than air as it clung to the ground like a mist and washed over the bodies.

"Do you think that stuff is dangerous?" asked Greg.

"Look," said Jonathan.

On the ground the mist had moved on past the third man and was slowly drifting into the centre of the facility. Something stirred close to the building, it was the first soldier. It looked like his foot was shaking, but then his entire body convulsed and he shuddered and stood up.

Greg stumbled backwards into the bed of the truck.

"Fuck me!" he shouted involuntarily.

The two men that were guarding the truck noticed him speaking and turned and one moved towards him.

"Shut the fuck up!" he shouted.

"Hey!" called the other guard as he tapped on his comrade's shoulder.

Turning around they faced the recently risen soldier who was staggering towards them. The first man lifted his M4 carbine and fired three rounds into the soldier's chest. The man spun and collapsed down, blood spurting from the chest wound. The guard turned and grinned to his comrade only to find another of the soldiers had his arm around his throat and was dragging him to the floor. The guard shouted for help and tumbled backwards, away from the fallen guard and his attacker.

More gunshots rang out as the bodies of the fallen men on both sides started to get up and stagger towards the living. Jackson wasted no time and moved to the side of the pick-up bed to try and cut the ropes on the exposed metalwork. It was slow work but with both guards and zombies running amok he had no choice. Ford and his group of guards emerged from the warehouse with the last of the patients. As they moved to the vehicles yet more of the recently risen zombies followed to attack them. Controlled and accurate fire from the men kept them out of danger, but the longer they stayed the greater the number of zombies.

"Sir!" shouted one of the men as the patient on the trolley started to convulse violently.

Ford stepped back just in time to see the person throw off his blanket and start shouting.

"What the hell is going on? Where am I?" he screamed.

One of the guards stepped forward to try and restrain him yet the man simply smashed his face with his fist. The force of the blow shocked Ford as he watched his guard fall to the ground with blood streaming from his face. The patient started to shake as though he was experiencing muscle spasms.

"What...have..you done to me?" he screamed before falling to the ground.

"Leave him!" shouted Ford as he ran on to the vehicles.

The front of the warehouse vanished in a bright blast that demolished its outer wall and anybody within twenty feet. Dust, debris and smoke blasted in all directions, including directly at the pickup truck that was smashed onto its side by the blast. Jackson was thrown violently against the body work, his head smashing into the bed before he passed out.

CHAPTER SIXTEEN

Decker and his unit rounded the corner of the street and approached the railway bridge with caution. In the distance they could all see the red glow of the warehouse. To make matters worse they could also hear the sound of a battle. A Toyota Corolla sped from a side street and narrowly avoided them before ploughing directly into one of the abandoned homes.

"What the hell's going on?" said Jason.

Along the street were small groups of people making their way away from the suburbs towards the seafront. It was hard to tell in the night light if they were running, walking or fleeing. Decker leaned over the side of the slow moving Unimog.

"What's going on?" he shouted.

The first person ignored him but the second, a woman in her thirties, called up to him.

"The creatures, they're here. They're all over the docks!" she shouted as she moved past.

"Creatures," shouted Tony, "she means the undead? They're here?"

A pickup truck came rushing down the road in their direction. As it drove past them they spotted a man firing a rifle back towards the docks.

"This doesn't look good does it!" observed Jason.

Decker banged on the crew cab to get the attention of the driver.

"Get us there fast!" he shouted before pulling out his radio.

"Decker here, we've got a serious problem. The dock area is compromised, we have a breach. I repeat, we have a breach," he said.

"Are you sure, Decker? If the facility is breached we will have to evacuate the entire island. I need you to confirm. We have a helicopter on its way to collect you. Get me intel and fast!" came back the reply from Dr Murphy back at the research station.

The Unimog trundled ever closer to the compound. They were now past the suburbs and approaching the entrance to the site. Up ahead was a damaged fence but there were no soldiers on duty. Off to the right were five trucks, all abandoned and one was burning. They kept moving towards the warehouse and the location of the brightest flames. The Unimog smashed through the fence and into the heart of the compound where an overturned pickup truck blocked their route. With a squeal the Unimog pulled to a halt. Decker was first out, quickly followed by his security unit.

Near the pickup were two men, one was trying to pull a man out from underneath the vehicle, the other was swinging a piece of metal at two attackers. Decker was experienced enough to know his attackers weren't soldiers, even though they were equipped as such. They moved with the stiffness and aggression he'd seen countless times before in his encounters with the undead.

"Secure the area, stay in sight of the Unimog and don't split up!" shouted Decker.

The small group fanned out so they could check the area, each man left no more than twenty feet between them. Decker ran over to the upturned pickup truck. As he moved he noted the number of undead shambling around, there must be at least two dozen, maybe more. Drawing his .45 he put three rounds into the closest, clearing a path to the vehicle. Up ahead he noticed the one man smash the piece of metal into the face of one of the zombies whilst another knocked him down. Decker ran forwards and kicked the creature, knocking it flat onto its back. He helped the man up.

"I'm Decker, need a hand?" he asked.

Around the truck more of the zombies congregated, each of them heading for the closest source of food. The man reached out and shook his hand.

"Jackson. Thanks. We need to get out of here!" he shouted.

"No shit!" said Decker. "What are you doing here?"

"Some guys were robbing the place, we got caught up in the middle," he answered.

Decker was unconvinced. He signalled over to Tony to give him a hand.

"Help them get this guy out, we need to get out of here and fast," he said.

Gunfire erupted from his unit as a group of zombies emerged from the direction of the road and the abandoned vehicles. His unit was well trained and half a dozen of them firing accurate bursts easily cut the group down.

Tony helped the two men to pull the wounded man from the truck.

"Anymore survivors?" asked Decker.

"Just Ford, I don't know where he went though," answered Jackson.

Decker dragged them in the direction of the Unimog.

"Come on, we need to go, now!" he shouted.

The two men in the cab of the Unimog jumped out, helping them to lift the injured man onto the back of the vehicle. The rest of the unit was already returning to the rear of the truck. Terry moved up to Decker.

"There are stretchers, trolleys and a few bodies. Looks like something pretty bad happened here," he said.

"Yeah, come on," replied Decker as he climbed up onto the back of the truck.

With a loud rev the Unimog reversed into the low wall and returned the route they'd arrived by. As they left the compound Decker watched the burning skyline. The zombies were on the move and in his experience they always found the living.

"Decker here, the compound is breached, they're in the open. I repeat they are in the open."

After a short pause an unfamiliar voice came back.

"Understood. Dr Murphy is on the evac chopper to the coast. We have reports across the city of sightings of the undead. We think the infection is spreading another way."

"What do you mean?" asked Decker.

Jackson leaned forwards.

"Yeah, we saw something leaking out of the warehouse. It turned the dead into zombies when it made contact with them," he said.

"You serious?" asked Tony.

"Bet your ass I'm serious, I saw three of them come back to life in front of me," he explained.

"We think the infection might be airborne," he said into the radio.

"One moment," came the reply. There was no response for almost twenty seconds.

"Decker, Murphy here. I'm on the way to the harbour.

Can you confirm the infection is airborne?" he asked.

"It looks that way, I didn't see any bites or injuries common with the usual spread of the infection on the zombies," he answered.

"Shit. Somebody must have damaged the containment tanks. The good news is the chemicals have a half life of approximately thirty days. The bad news is that means this site needs to be put into immediate quarantine," said Dr Murphy.

"Quarantine?" shouted an angry Decker.

"You know the drill. Anybody that has been in contact with the infection will have to wait it out. In six months the airborne virus will be impotent."

The Unimog shook as it took a turn too fast and clipped a road sign. Its weight and mass slammed it past the debris and it ploughed on towards the harbour.

"We're leaving the island in thirty minutes. We have already sent an SOS to the flotilla. The RV Moreau is under three hundred miles away and on her way to assist. Get to our vessel, the Colossus by then or be left behind. Understood?" said Dr Murphy.

"Affirmative," answered Decker.

He moved up so that he could see over the top of the cab. In was incredible, in such a short amount of time the peaceful island was already in chaos. Fires were burning off to the left and people were in the streets, heading for the evacuation zones at the harbour. Decker was almost thrown into the cab as the Unimog screeched to a halt. He leaned over, shouting at the driver.

"What's wrong?" he called.

The driver pointed out into the street ahead. Decker climbed up higher to get a better view. Two trucks were overturned in the street and around them were at least two dozen bodies.

Jackson climbed up, watching ahead.

"Yeah, that looks like the trucks Ford came in. He's the one that let them out," he said.

Decker looked at him with a little suspicion.

"Are you sure that's his vehicles?"

"Pretty sure," he answered.

A volley of shots came from the back of the Unimog as the men spotted zombies approaching from behind.

"Decker! Come on!" shouted Tony.

Decker moved back to check, the zombies were growing in substantial numbers and were hell bent on attacking those of them that were still left.

"Where are they coming from?" asked a confused Decker.

"Well, if it's airborne, is it affecting anybody that's dead? What about the living?" said Tony.

Decker shrugged.

A hand appeared on the side of the Unimog, a sound of a desperate man cried out.

"Help me, they're everywhere," he yelled before being

pulled back down.

Jason leaned over to try and help only to be grabbed by the waiting hands of a dozen zombies. He tried to hold on but they were too many and in seconds he was on the ground being bitten and torn apart.

"Fuck!" shouted Decker as he fired round after round into the group, making sure his first round put the mortally wounded Jason out of his misery.

The rest of the group fired in all directions as yet more and more of the undead appeared, all staggering towards the immobile Unimog. Decker banged on the cab.

"Push past them!" he screamed whilst firing straight ahead at the approaching zombies.

With a roar the Unimog lurched forwards and towards the two wrecked trucks that blocked the road. With a crash they smashed into the wrecks and pushed past surprisingly easily. With the engine revving hard they were back onto their journey.

Decker turned back to the rest of his group.

"Make sure you're ready. We are gonna hit the ground running, understood?"

They all nodded and Decker climbed back to the rear of the cab, watching the harbour area coming closer and closer to them. Tony got up and joined him, passing several magazines.

"Thanks," said Decker.

Up ahead, crowds of people were filling the streets and

heading for the shore. The emergency klaxons fitted days after the outbreak were all blaring, warning people to stay indoors, not that anybody was paying them any attention. The Unimog pushed on down the street, the jetties now clear in the distance.

"Decker!" shouted Tony as he waved his arms off to the right.

Decker turned, tracking the movement till he spotted the problem. Two pickup trucks were approaching three blocks ahead and to the right. They were obviously heading in the same direction and would cut into their path shortly. The rattle of weapons fire blasted ahead.

"The bastards are shooting the civvies!" shouted Jackson.

Decker watched, his face showing the anger he felt as the two trucks mowed down dozens of helpless people trying to get along the road. He opened the rear hatch and popped his head into the cab.

"We need to get in front of those bastards!" he said pointing at the junction ahead. "If they get to the boat first we're screwed."

The driver nodded and changed gear, moving the lumbering truck at a slightly higher speed. The junction was now only a block away and yet more people were filling the road. The driver held down the air horn, making the people jump out of the way.

"Look!" shouted Greg as he waved off to their left. He

picked up one of the rifles from the back of the truck and aimed it off into the distance.

"I see them, a group of about thirty zombies are coming from the industrial units. You see them?" he asked.

"Yeah," said Decker, "drop them!"

The men opened fire on any zombies they could see. In a short time the creatures seemed to be spreading across the island faster than at any time he'd ever seen. The Unimog sped past the junction, Decker could see the approaching trucks were a block away and moving fast. Out in front of them the sound of ship horns blared as vessels moved away from the coast.

"Shit!" shouted Tony, are there gonna be any left for us?"

The Doctor promised the Colossus would be waiting for another..." he checked his watch, "seven minutes."

The trucks were now on the same stretch of road and accelerating towards them.

"What the fuck are they doing?" said Decker.

"No way!" shouted Jackson. "I know those trucks, it's Ford."

Jonathan still dazed from the incident back at the warehouse got up to look back. He muttered to Jackson.

"If that's Ford he'll fuck us for good," he said before slumping back down.

"He's right," said Jackson, "he doesn't care who suffers as long as he gets what he wants."

Bright lights flashed from the approaching trucks and Jonathan flew back against the cab, his torso was riddled with bullet holes.

"Fuck!" shouted Jackson.

The rest of the men ducked down low and returned fire. The one truck stayed behind them whilst the second sped to their right and moved alongside the Unimog. Luckily for Decker the lumbering Mercedes was substantially taller and from their vantage point they could bring fire down on the hapless criminals firing from the bed of the truck.

They fired long bursts from their carbines into the men, killing two and blasting a third off the back and into the street before the truck was able to speed past. Behind them the other truck rushed at them and slammed into the back of the Unimog. With a sickening crunch it jerked forward but its mass kept it moving on.

They might have made it, apart from the fact that the overtaking pickup truck clipped an abandoned car just as it moved ahead. The impact spun its rear outwards and directly into the path of the Unimog. This time mass wasn't enough and the Unimog slid first to the right and then as the driver overcompensated it tipped over onto its side. Because of the speed they were travelling the overturned truck slid a good hundred yards before coming to a stop. Right behind it the other pickup swerved to avoid the crash only to pile straight into one of the homes that ran along the road and disappeared inside in a cloud of metal, dust and debris.

* * *

Jackson was the first to drag himself out of the wreckage. There were bodies all around the crash site. Some of them he recognised, others he didn't. As he checked the back of the Unimog for survivors a burst of gunfire sent him diving for the ground. From the side of the road a man approached, flanked by an armed guard. The man wore a suit and upon approaching a wounded man simply pointed the weapon at the man's head and fired.

"Fuck," muttered Jackson as he crawled through the wreckage.

The sound of metal being dropped signalled the driver was trying to climb out of the cab of the Unimog. He was half out when another burst of fire caught him in the chest, he slumped back inside. Jackson tried to slide back to the wreckage but he was too slow, the man approached and stood in front of him.

"Jackson, my, oh my, you got this far?" he laughed.

You bastard!" shouted Jackson. "Why?"

"I have my own experiments," he answered, whilst scanning the distant jetties to make sure the boat was still there. He then looked at his watch.

"Looks like you're going to miss the last boat, too bad," he said as he raised his pistol.

A loud crack blasted next to Jackson's face and Ford staggered backwards. Jackson turned to see Decker kneeling and holding out his automatic. Ford's guard returned fire managing to hit Decker in the leg. He fell back in pain, dropping the pistol. Jackson stood up and smashed into the guard, knocking both men to the ground. He may have caught him by surprise, but the guard was stronger and more experienced and quickly spun him around and forced his arm into a painful lock.

"Hey!" shouted Decker who was now pointing his recovered pistol at the man.

The guard turned only to be hit in the face by a single round from the gun.

"That's two you owe me!" grinned Decker before dropping to his knee.

"Where's Ford?" shouted Jackson.

Decker shrugged, whilst Jackson staggered around the crash site looking for signs of survivors. It was incredible, but in the crash and ensuing massacre by Ford, it seemed only the two men and Ford were left.

A young family ran past carrying an array of bags on their backs. Jackson tried to stop one only to be pushed back

"Get off me, they're here!" screamed the woman.

Jackson turned to see the growing horde making its way down the road and towards the waterfront.

"Shit, come on man, we need to go!" he shouted.

He moved over to Decker and helped him up before spotting movement inside the back of the wrecked Unimog. The two men moved over slowly, peering inside. A hand came out quickly followed by the familiar wail of the undead. It was a man, somehow he had turned without being bitten.

Jackson pushed the man back whilst Decker hesitated before putting two rounds into the walking corpse. The two then staggered off down the street and towards the last remaining vessel.

"It must be airborne then, that's a problem, a pretty serious one!" said Decker.

"No shit," muttered Jackson as they reached the end of the road and the entrance to the jetties.

Jackson and Decker carried on down the promenade towards the jetties that reached out to the various vessels tied up. In the distance was the shape of the Colossus, a converted pleasure boat that was used to move supplies around the islands. The engine was running from the amount of smoke belching from its engines, and there were dozens of people already onboard.

Jackson jumped over the security fence and turned back to help the injured Decker. Off to their right a group of the undead smashed out of an outbuilding and made their way towards the men.

"Come on!" screamed Jackson, as he emptied the last of his bullets from his MP7 at the group.

The bullets thudded away at the group but it seemed to do little to reduce the numbers. Decker was at the top of the fence and Jackson, now running short on patience simply grabbed his arm and yanked him over and down to the ground. He landed with a thud. Behind the two men the horde had increased to hundreds of zombies and they were all heading in the same direction as them, the boat.

Jackson pulled Decker up and put his arm around his neck to help take the weight. The two then staggered off down the jetty towards the boat.

A scream came from up ahead as someone fell from the boat. Several gunshots rang out before Decker spotted the group of five zombies fighting their way off the jetty onto the boat. More gunshots rang out as people tried to jump onboard. The engines revved loudly and more smoke poured from the oily engines.

The two men carried on as quickly as they could, the boat was now only about a hundred yards away. Jackson, moving too quickly, stumbled and fell hard onto the ground. Decker toppled and collapsed next to him. The closest zombies were only twenty feet away and had already blocked their route back from the jetty.

Decker pulled out his automatic pistol and slammed in another clip. With expert marksmanship he emptied the clip, one aimed round after another whilst Jackson stood up and waved at the vessel to wait. With a roar a plume of water sprayed from the rear of the boat as the propellers kicked up water. The boat pushed ahead slowly from the jetty.

"What the fuck!" shouted Decker as he kneeled on the ground, still shooting.

Jackson ran over to him, helping him up to his feet and drawing his own pistol and aiming down the jetty at the approaching horde. Behind them the sound of the Colossus was already quietening at it steamed out to its rendezvous with the Moreau.

"This place is going to hell!" screamed Jackson as he opened fire.

THE END

Lightning Source UK Ltd.
Milton Keynes UK
29 December 2010

164963UK00001B/116/P